Spin

by

CD Reiss

Songs of Corruption – Book One

D1714463

Chapter 1.

Oh, Jonathan.

I mentally rolled my eyes, if such a thing were possible, and kept my physical eyes focused on the woman singing. She had a lovely voice. It wasn't quite like a bird, but more like a dozen of them layered one on top of the other. The effect was hypnotic.

I glanced at my brother again. "Excuse me?"

"Yeah?"

"You just agreed that the Angels were superior to the Dodgers."

He looked away from her, and I sensed the air between them rip. I hadn't felt anything but annoyance with his lack of attentiveness until he looked at me again, and his entire face changed from voracious and single-minded to the usual bemused and arrogant.

"This season?"

"Are you even paying attention?" I asked.

"Look, you have six sisters and me. All your sisters will tell you to forget Daniel Brower completely. I'm telling you to forgive him if you have to, but if you're going to, just do it and drop it. I'm the one you keep talking to about him, and I keep giving you the same answer. So it sounds like you want to go back to him."

He was in love with his ex-wife, who had left him for another man. Of course he'd be the most forgiving, and of course he was the one I chose to be with.

"I can't. Every time I look at him, I can't stop seeing him having sex with that girl."

"Don't look at him."

I folded my hands on the table. I shouldn't see my ex. Ever. But he'd called, and I had lunch with him, like a damned fool. He'd said it was business, and in a way, it was. We had a mortgage together, and bills, and I knew the intimacies of his campaign for mayor about as well as I'd known the intimacies of his body. But with so much dead weight between us, I had trouble eating. In the end, of course, he'd asked for me back, and I'd declined while holding back tears.

"He keeps asking to see me," I said.

"Jesus Christ, Theresa. He's stringing you along." Jonathan tipped his drink to his lips and watched the woman standing by the piano like a hawk observing a mouse. "I thought I had it bad."

I felt a sudden ball of tension wrap up in my chest. I couldn't exactly place it, but it irritated me. "Do you know her? The singer."

"We have a thing later tonight."

"Good, because I was going to say you might want to introduce yourself before you slobber on her. Maybe dinner and a show."

He smiled a big, wide Jonathan grin. After his wife left, he'd turned into a womanizing prick, but he rarely let us see that side of him. He was always a gentleman, until I saw him look at that singer. It made me uncomfortable. Not because he was my brother, which should have been enough, but because of an uneasy, empty feeling I chased away.

"Go to Tahoe or something for a few weeks," he said. "Slap some skis on. You're giving yourself an ulcer."

"I'm fine."

The musicians stopped, and people clapped. She *was* good. My brother just applauded with his eyes and tipped his glass to her. When she saw him, her jaw tightened with anger. Apparently, he knew her well enough to piss her off.

He leaned over and whispered in my ear, "I know damn well how not fine you are."

I looked him square in the eyes, and I knew his hurt matched mine. He healed himself by seducing whoever he fancied. I didn't think I could use the same strategy. It stopped mattering when the singer made a beeline for our table.

"Hi, Jonathan," she said, a big, fake smile draped across her face.

"Monica," he said. "This is Theresa."

"That was beautiful," I said.

"Thanks."

"You were incredible," Jonathan said. "I've never heard anything like that."

"I've never heard of a man trying to sandwich another woman between fingering me and fucking me in the same day."

I almost spit out my Cosmo. Jonathan laughed. I felt sorry for the girl. She looked as if she was going to cry. I hated my brother just then. Hated him with a dogged vehemence because not only was he messing with her feelings, he still looked at her as though he wanted to eat her alive. When I saw how she looked at him, I knew he would win. He would have her and a dozen others, and she wouldn't even know what was happening. I couldn't watch.

"I'm going to the ladies'," I said and slid out of the booth, not looking back.

I leaned against the back of the stall, staring at the single strip of toilet paper dangling off the roll. I had a few squares in my bag, just in case my brother brought me to yet another dump, but I didn't want to use them. I wanted to dig into that feeling of emptiness and find the bottom of it.

You always have a few squares in your bag. And two Advil. And a tampon.

Daniel's voice listing the stuff I carried for emergencies; his face, smiling as we went out the door for some charity thing; him in a tux, me in something, holding a satin clutch into which a normal woman couldn't fit more than a tube of lipstick and a raisin.

"You got your whole kit in there?" he'd asked.

"Of course."

"Space and time are your slaves."

I'd been pleased at the way he looked at me, as if he couldn't be more impressed and proud, as if I ruled the world and his servitude was the natural order. Pleased as a king opening a pie and finding the miracle of four-and-twenty blackbirds.

But though I'd been with him for seven years, he'd never looked at me the way Jonathan looked at that singer. Never. Maybe that was why Daniel had had sex with his speechwriter. He didn't revere her; he fucked her.

Daniel had always called me Tink, short for Tinkerbell, because of my curvy, petite frame. A sprightly, delicate fairy. Not someone you looked at hungrily.

I saw the singer in the hall, looking distant and resolute at the same time, as if she was convincing herself of something. She stopped short when she saw me.

"I'm so sorry," she said. "I was rude and unbecoming."

I was going to deny it, but I was struck by a distraction that cut me to the core. I smelled pine trees, deep in the forest, damp in the morning after a night of campfires and singing. The burning char and dew mingled in the song-like trails of cigarette smoke, rising and disappearing. And then it was gone.

"My brother's an asshole, so I don't blame you." I regretted that almost immediately. I didn't talk like that, especially not about family. I took her hand and squeezed it. "We both loved your voice."

"Thank you. I have to go. I'll try to see you on the way out." She slipped her hand away and walked toward the dressing room.

I caught the scent again and looked in her direction, as if I could see the smell's source. It could have come from anyone. It could have been the gorgeous black lady with the sweet smile. It could have been the plate of saucy meat that crossed my path. Could have been the waft of parking lot that came through the door before it snapped closed.

But it wasn't.

I knew it like I knew tax code; it was him. The man in the dark suit and thin pink tie, the full lips and two-day beard. His eyes were black as a felony, and they stayed on me as his body swung into the booth.

The smell had come from him, not the other man getting into the booth. It was in his gaze, which was locked on me, disarming me. He was beautiful to me. Not my type, not at all. But the slight cleft in his chin, the powerful jaw, the swoop of dark hair falling over his forehead seemed right. Just *right*. I swallowed. My mouth had started watering, and my throat had gotten dry. I got a flash of him above me, with that swoop of hair rocking, as he fucked me so hard the sheets ripped.

He turned to say something to the hostess, and I took a gulp of air. I'd forgotten to breathe. I put my hands to my shirt buttons to make sure they were fastened, because I felt as if he'd undressed me.

I had two ways to return to Jonathan: behind the piano, which was the crowded, shorter way, or in front, which was less populated but longer.

I walked in front of the piano. The less crowded way. The longer way. The way that took me right past the man in the pink tie.

I wanted him to look at me, and he spent the entire length of our proximity talking earnestly to the baby-faced, bow-lipped man next to him. I caught the burned, dewy pine scent that made no sense and kept walking.

I felt a tug on my wrist, a warm sensation that tingled. His hand was on me, gentle but resolved. I stopped, looking at him as his hand brought me to his face. He drew me down until he was whisper close. A sudden rush of potential went from the back of my neck to the space between my legs, waking me where I thought I'd died.

I couldn't breathe.

I couldn't speak.

If he kissed me, I would have opened my mouth for him. That, I knew for sure.

"Your shoe," he said with an accent I couldn't place.

"What?" I couldn't stop looking at his eyes: brown, wide, with longer eyelashes than should be legal, hooded under arched brows proportioned for expression.

Was I wearing shoes? Was I standing? Did I need to take in air? Eat? Or could I just live off the energy between us?

He pointed at my heel. "You brought yourself a souvenir from the ladies' room."

He was beautiful, even as he smirked with those full lips. Did I have to turn away to see what he was talking about? It was that or put my tongue down his throat. I looked down.

I had a trail of toilet paper on my stiletto.

"Thank you," I said.

"My pleasure." He let go of my hand.

The space where he'd touched felt like a missed opportunity, and I went to the bathroom to return my souvenir.

Chapter 2.

After I'd kicked Daniel out of my loft, Katrina moved in. Living alone had thrust me hip deep into depression, and her things around the house changed my feeling of complete emptiness into a feeling that something was right even when everything was wrong.

For her part, she was dealing with a career that had crashed and burned when she filed a lawsuit against the studio that had funded her Oscar-nominated movie. She said there were profits she was entitled to share; they insisted the production operated at a loss. Fancy, indefensible, and legal accounting proved them right, leaving her bank account empty and her career in tatters.

She and I were cars passing on opposite sides of the freeway. As a nearly-but-not-quite-famous director, she was on set at odd hours, and when she wasn't, she was trying to hold her production together with spit and chewing gum. She couldn't pay much, so her crew left for scale-paying gigs and had to be replaced, or they dropped out of a day's shooting with grave apologies but no replacement. Set designers, assistant camera people, gaffers did it for love and opportunity. Production assistants, also called PAs, were the unskilled and barely paid necessities on set, and most likely to drop out.

Her script supervisor, the person responsible for the continuity of the shots, couldn't work nights or weekends. After Katrina fired her line producer, who was in charge of keeping ducks in rows, she discovered he hadn't hired a second script supervisor.

She shrugged it off as the risk one takes in "the business," then segued into a long pitch about my attention to detail, my love of consistency and order, and my eagle eye for continuity. She'd asked—no, begged—me to step in for evenings and weekends.

I met her on set under a viaduct downtown at six a.m. The food truck was set up, and the gaffers and grips were just arriving.

"Let's face it, Tee Dray," she said, pointing the straw of her Big Gulp at me, "it's not like they gave me enough money to pay union for weekend calls." She wore a baseball cap over a tight black pixie cut that only she could pull off. A Vietnamese Mexican with an athletic build, she carried herself as if she owned the joint. Every joint. When we were at Carlton Prep together, she was a bossy outcast and the most interesting person at school.

"You're paying me on the back end," I said.

"Sure," she said with a strong smile. "Forty percent, but I keep the books."

We hovered over the coffee and fruit. It was still dark, the ambient hiss of the freeway above as low as it would ever be.

"You know what to do?" she asked.

"I have the binder from last time. Track shots, cuts, who's wearing what, where their hands are, off-book dialogue, et cetera."

"I really appreciate this," she said.

"You deserve a comeback. I'd finance the whole thing, you know."

"Then I'd feel obligated to sleep with you." She winked. A flirtatious bisexual, she'd offered herself to me more than once, joking, then not, then joking again.

"I think I'm getting to the point I'd take you up on it," I joked back.

We'd lost touch during college then reconnected when she got representation at WDE, where I ran the client accounting department. She had directed an action movie with heart and suspense that filled theaters for months. It was in the lexicon of greats, nominated for awards, watched and rewatched years after release. When she'd lost her contract with Overland Studios because of her lawsuit, I knew all the intimate fiscal details because I worked for her agent. She could cry on my shoulder or vent her frustration without explaining the nuances of studio math, or as she called it, ass-rape on a ledger.

A studio like Overland loaned a production company money to make a film then billed themselves interest. The interest compounded for the months of production then into the years following release until a blockbuster like Katrina's wound up with no profits. No amount of litigation could erase the foul and totally legal practice.

Her current self-made episodic piece, to be shot in diners and under viaducts, was financed through a tiny holding in Qatar. Written, directed, and produced by Katrina Ip, it could put her back on the map. I couldn't have rooted harder for anyone's success.

"You need a man," she said. "A rebound cock to fuck the sad right out of you."

"Nice way to talk."

"The truth isn't always nice. Let me set you up with my brother, and you can set me up with yours."

"You don't have a brother."

"Can't blame a girl for trying. What about Michael?" She raised an eyebrow, tilting her head. The lead actor in the production had made it clear he was interested in me and a couple of other attractive women on set. He was a man whore, but a nice one.

"I'm not ready," I said.

"I know, sweetheart. It'll come back. Some time."

I pressed my lips together, and though the sun was just peeking over the skyline, it was light enough for her to see the prickly heat brush my cheeks.

"Theresa," she said, "call is in four minutes. I'm going to have no time to talk. So tell me now. And fast."

It was a miracle we'd even had time to talk already. Directing a movie was like having a wedding every day for four months. You threw the party but couldn't enjoy it.

"I went out with Jonathan last night, and there was a guy. A man. I had toilet paper on my shoe and—"

"You? Miss Perfect?"

"Yes. I was so embarrassed." I dropped my voice to a near whisper when Edgar, her assistant director, approached with a clipboard and a problem. "He was breathtaking."

She leaned on one hip. "Los Angeles is wall-to-wall breathtaking."

"He was different. When he touched me—"

"He touched you?"

"Just my wrist. But it was like sex. I swear I've never felt anything like that."

"You tell me this *now?*"

Edgar got within earshot, and I dropped my eyes. Even thinking about that man in range of a stranger made me feel shameful.

"Kat," Edgar spoke fast, "honey, the LAPD—"

"Give them the forms," she shot back.

"But they—"

"Can wait five minutes." She pulled me behind a trailer. The hum of the generator almost drowned her out. "You cried on my lap for hours over Danny Dickhead. Now you have a hundred-twenty seconds to tell me about this new one."

"There's nothing to tell."

"I will cut you." She didn't mean it, of course. Even coming from the wrong side of Pico Boulevard, her threats were all affect.

"Brown eyes. Black hair."

"You must be off blonds since Dickerino Boy."

"Six feet. Built. My god, his hands. They weren't narrow or soft. They were wide, and... I'm not making any sense. But when he looked at me, my skin went hot. All I could think about was... you know."

"You got a number?"

"Not even a name."

Her phone dinged, and three people approached at once. Her day had begun. She turned away from me but flipped her head back. "You just got woken up."

Chapter 3.

Ten years ago, I couldn't have gotten a donut three blocks away from my loft without getting jacked. In Los Angeles at the turn of the second millennia, the wealthy moved from the city's perimeter back to the center. And if anyone was "the wealthy," it was me.

We lived in an old corset and girdle factory. It had been abandoned in the sixties, used as a warehouse by a stonecutter and cabinet maker, then expanded and converted into lofts just before the Great Recession. The units had gone at fire sale prices. I could afford whatever I needed, but Daniel had insisted on paying half, and the recession hit him hard. So a short sale downtown loft at a million and change it was.

And I was stuck with it. He moved to Mar Vista after I kicked him out, and I commuted across town to Beverly Hills to run client accounting at WDE.

Studios did not cut checks to talent; they cut checks to their agents. The agents deducted their ten percent fee and sent the client the rest. Thus, Hollywood agencies were the beating heart of the industry, the nexus through which all money circulated.

And most of them were still cutting paper checks.

I'd been hired to move the company from paper to wire transfer, and I'd done it. I'd convinced old guard agents, grizzled actors, below the line talent, banks, and business managers to get into the twenty-first century. Many of our clients still insisted on bike-messengered and armored-trucked paper checks, but they were more and more the minority. New clients weren't given a paper option.

I was still necessary to manage the rest of the paper trail, chase studios for payment, and run the department, but I felt my job was done. The only thing worse than the idea of living with my job was the idea of living without it, of drifting into a life without purpose. My sister Fiona had made an art form of it in her youth, and I'd watched her slip into debauchery. I'd do anything to not be her.

But there I was, closing my eyes and seeing those hated checks. I heard the tones of my follow-up call to the messenger service, the *tip tap* as Pam logged them in one by one, and I thought, *I want to burn it all and then slip into oblivion.* I never did. I dreamed about it sometimes while I spaced off looking at the numbers or listening to one of the agents throw his anxiety on the table when a client's check was a day late.

I thought about law school then dismissed the idea. If I became a lawyer as well as an accountant, I'd be so valuable I'd be miserable.

"Hey, Fly Girl." Gene stood over my desk. "Rolf Wente's business manager needs you to follow up with Warner's."

I tapped my phone log. "We have calls out to them."

"You look tired. How was the weekend? Do the whole party thing?"

If I didn't answer, and if I wasn't specific, he'd spend fifteen minutes telling me about his party habits. "Went to dinner the other night. We saw this lounge act. The singer was terrific. Faulkner. Something Faulkner. Like the writer."

"Never heard of her," he said.

"Nice voice. Original."

"Whyncha send me the deets? Maybe we'll get out there on the WDE dime. Bring the assistants. Make them feel loved."

"Okay." I turned back to my work, hoping he'd leave.

"And get on Warner's, okay? We lose old Rolf, and we're up the ass on the dry highway. Let me know about the singer by the end of day."

I didn't realize that by suggesting a musician, I was obligated to ride the company dime to yet another show at Frontage. I was exhausted even thinking about it, until I remembered the man with the pink tie. I grabbed my phone and went outside.

I walked by Barney's. It was bridal month, apparently. High end designers had their white gowns in the window. Jeremy St. James had a jewel-encrusted corset over a skirt no more modest than a strip of gauze. Barry Tilden layered dove white feathers on skirt worthy of Scarlet O'Hara, topping it all with a bodice made purely of silver zippers.

"Deirdre?" I said when I heard her pick up. "You there?"

"What time is it?"

"Ten. What are you doing next Thursday night?"

Sheets rustled. "I have to be at the shelter late."

"Wanna go out?"

"I can't do anything fancy, Tee. It makes me sick." My sister Deirdre despised the consumptions of the rich. She lived in a studio the size of a postage stamp and put every penny of her trust fund interest toward feeding the hungry. It was noble to the point of self-destruction.

"It's not fancy. Kind of dumpy. I don't want to go with just work people. They all look at me like they're sorry for me about Daniel. I hate it."

"I'm not a good buffer."

"You're perfect. You keep me on my toes."

She sighed. "All right. You're buying, though. I'm broke."

"No problem."

We hung up, and I fist-pumped the ivory Sartorial Sandwich in the last window. I needed Deirdre there to give me a reason to escape the WDE crowd, especially if the breathtaking man was there.

Chapter 4.

"How many have you had?" I asked Deirdre.

"My second." She took her hand off her mop of curly red hair to hold up two fingers. All eight of us shared the red hair, but only she had the curls. "Not that it matters."

"It matters," I said.

"No," Deirdre said, putting down her glass. "It doesn't. Do you know what matters?"

"Let me guess. The poor and hungry?"

Deirdre huffed. I'd caught her before she could make her speech. She hated that. "You've got more money than the Vatican. You're cute as a button. Yet you think you have problems."

"Looks and money aren't the whole of a person."

"Don't pretend they don't matter. They do. If you saw what I saw every day."

My sister was sweet and compassionate, but she was a belligerent drunk. If I let her, she'd tell me my sadness came from material idolatry and that it was time for me to give all my money to charity and live in service to the poor. I'd often considered the possibility that she was right.

The musicians had come by and then disappeared again. The lights dimmed, and she appeared by the piano singing "Stormy Weather" as if she wanted to rip the clouds from the sky but couldn't reach high enough. Monica Faulkner, a nobody singer in a town of somebodies, stood in front of the piano singing other people's songs in a room built for other purposes. She moved from "Stormy Weather" to something more plaintive. My God, she was fully committed to every word, every note.

There was no halfway with that woman. I'd seen her sandwiched between my brother fingering her and fucking her, and I'd felt bad. But not today, she had control over me. She sang in the tempo of keys clacking and printers humming. There was an open place inside me, past where the professionalism cracked and the weariness fissured and the sadness throbbed. She caressed that place then jabbed it.

I missed Daniel. I missed the hardness of his body and the touch of his hands. I missed his laughter, and the way he cupped my breast in his sleep, and the weight of his arm on my shoulder, and the way he brushed his light brown hair off his face. I missed calling him to tell him where I was. I was an independent woman. I could function fine without him or anyone. But I missed him, and I missed being loved. Once he'd cheated on me, all my delight in his love drowned in bitterness. I was wistful for something dead.

"You all right?" said a male voice.

Gene had left the table to come talk to me at the bar. He was my "type": dark blonde, straight-laced, ambitious, easy smile, confident. But he was awful. Just the most awful Hollywood douchebag.

"Yeah, thanks."

"She's good. The singer. "

"Great." I felt an absence to my right, where Deirdre had been standing.

"I think we could do something with her. Little spit and polish, shorter skirt. Use the body. Sammy's got Geraldine Stark under contract. She's trying to move into fashion. Could be a tight package." He winked as if I might not get his double entendre.

"I hope it works out," I said. "I'm off to the ladies'."

"See you back at the table." He picked up his glass. "Don't be a stranger."

Deirdre wasn't in the bathroom. I ended up looking at the same roll of toilet paper from two weeks ago. Still one square hanging. A different roll, obviously, but the same amount. Not enough.

Just not enough.

The hall outside the bathroom led outside, where a little seating area with ashtrays was blocked off from the parking lot. I heard yelling and repeated calls of "bitch." Though I normally avoided disagreeable behavior, I went to look.

A red Porsche Boxster was parked in the handicapped spot, and on the hood, all five-eleven, hundred-and-fifty pounds of her, Deirdre sprawled on her back. The man yelling was six inches shorter and twenty pounds lighter—if I didn't count the weight of the petroleum in his hair products. He wore head-to-toe leather and had a voice like a car screeching to a halt.

"Get. Off. The. Porsche." He pushed her as he yelled, but she was dead weight.

"Excuse me," I said.

He may have heard me. I had no time to think about that; the rest happened so fast. He pulled at Deirdre's lapels, yanking her forward. Like a baby with a bellyful of milk, she projectile vomited. It splashed on his jacket, the ground, and the car. He squealed and let her go. She rolled off the hood, puking as she went, and landed on the ground.

"Fuck!" he yelled as I tried to sit my sister up against the wheel. "Shit. God. Puke? Puke is acid! Do you know what that's going to do to the paint? And my fucking jacket?"

"We'll pay for the damage."

I was too busy with Deirdre to bother looking at the creep. She was unconscious. I squeezed her cheeks and looked into her mouth to see if she was choking. She wasn't, because she threw up right down my shirt. I leaned back and said something like *ugh,* but it was drowned out by the man in leather.

"This is a custom paint job. Fuck! Bitch, the *whole car's* gotta be redone. And I got a thing tomorrow."

"Sorry," I mumbled, tapping Deirdre's cheek.

If he hadn't been blinded by his rage and stupidity, Leather Guy probably wouldn't have done what he did in front of me.

Holding his arms so they didn't touch the puke on his chest, he came around the car and kicked Deirdre in the hip.

"Hey!" was all I got to say.

I didn't even have a chance to stand and challenge him before he fell back as if an airplane door had opened mid-flight. Then I heard a bang. I looked back at Deirdre, because in my panic, I thought she'd fallen or gotten hit by a car.

A voice, gentle yet sharp, said, "Does she drink like this often?" A blue-eyed man with a young face and bow lips crouched beside me. He didn't look at me but at Deirdre. "I think she's got alcohol poisoning."

Another bang. I jumped. A splash of vomit landed on my cheek, and I looked up at the hood of the car. Leather's cheek was pressed against the hood of the Porsche.

"Spin," Bow Lips said, "take it easy, would you?"

Above him, with his arm pinning down Leather's face, was the breathtaking man, ignoring his friend. "Tell this lady you're sorry."

"He should apologize to my sister, not me," I said.

"Fuck you!" The douchebag wiggled. He got thumped against the hood for his trouble. "I ain't saying shit."

Spin pulled Leather up by his collar and slammed his face on the hood until he screamed.

"I'll call 9-1-1," said Bow Lips.

"But I—" *I thought you were this guy's friend.* I stopped myself, realizing he was going to call about Deirdre, not the creep getting his face slammed against a car.

"Say. You're. Sorry," Spin said through his teeth.

Leather's face slid to the edge of the hood, wiping puke, until I could see the blood and paint-shredding stomach acid mixing on his cheeks from my crouching position. He spit a little blood.

He was a douchebag and he'd kicked my sister, but I felt bad for him. "It's okay, really, I—"

"Yeah, we have an emergency." Bow Lips. Unflustered. Into the phone "Alcohol poisoning."

Bang.

"I'm sorry!"

"Do you believe him, *Contessa*?" Beautiful. Even beating the hell out of some guy on the hood of a Porsche. "Do you think he's sorry?"

I caught a hint of an accent in his voice. Italian? He was speaking to me, one eyebrow arched like a parabola, his face closed with resolve, impassioned with purpose, yet calm, as if he was so good at what he did he didn't need to break a sweat.

"Yes," I said, "I believe him."

"I believe he regrets it," he said. "But I don't believe he's remorseful." He leaned toward me on the owner of the Porsche, who was crying through a bloody nose. "What do you think?"

I don't know what came over me. The need to be truthful turned me and that gorgeous man into cohorts. It was intimate in a safe way, and the creep in leather needed to suffer. "No, I don't think he is."

His smirk lit up the night. I feared a full-on smile might put me over the edge.

"Show her you mean it," he said in Leather's ear but looked at me. "Get the puke off this ugly fucking car." He wouldn't let the guy move. "Get it off."

"Female," Bow Lips said, all business. "Mid thirties. Built like a brick shithouse."

"Lick that shit up, or you're kissing the hood again."

Leather choked and sobbed, blood pouring from his nose. I stood up and looked at the guy who had kicked my sister. I felt something pouring off the two men locked together on the car. Heat. Energy. Something that crawled under my skin and made it tingle. And when the creep stuck his tongue out and licked the vomit off the hood, the tingle turned to a release from anxiety I hadn't realized I carried.

"That's right," Spin said. "You believe him now, Contessa?"

"Yes."

Spin yanked the man up, and I knew from the look on his face that he was going to make the guy kiss the hood again. The distance and force applied would not just break, but smash bones.

I stood. "I think you've made your point."

Spin's face, so implacable, breached into something gentler, more open, as if an understanding reached not his intelligence, but his adrenal glands. He smiled. "I thought you'd enjoy a big ending."

"My sister will be bruised. His face is cracked open. Justice is served."

"*Come volevi tu*," he said, yanking the creep back again. "Keys." He held out his hand as Leather cried, tears streaking the mass of blood.

"No, man, don't take my car."

"This car?" He pulled the keys out of Leather's pocket and hit a button. The doors unlocked, and the lights flashed. "You're taking this low-class piece-of-shit car out of my sight." He pushed the man inside and closed the door.

In a few seconds, the car started and screeched away.

"Ambulance coming," Bow Lips said from behind me, his voice strained.

He had stood Deirdre up and was about to fall under her dead weight. His friend intervened and helped carry her to the smokers' benches. From inside, I heard clapping. The singer was done. People would come out for their cigarettes soon. The breathtaking man pulled the sleeves of his jacket straight and touched his tie. Nothing was out of place.

"You okay?" I asked.

"Yes. You?" He took a pack of cigarettes from his pocket and offered me one.

I refused with a tilt of my head. I glanced at Deirdre, who leaned against Bow Lips. He'd need to be rescued.

"I'm fine. Covered in throw up, but fine," I said.

"You didn't get upset, seeing that. I'm impressed." He poked out a smoke and bit the end, sliding it out of its sardine-tight box while absently fingering a silver lighter.

"Oh, I'm upset."

He smiled as he lit up, looking at me over the flame. He snapped the lighter shut with a loud click, taking his time. I had a second to run and sit next to my sister, take a step back. But I didn't.

"You don't look upset," he said. "You're flushed. Your heart is racing. I can see it." He stepped forward. "Your breath, you're trying to control it. But it's not working. If I saw you like this in a different time or place, I'd think you were ready to fuck."

Just watching me, he let the smoke rise in a white miasma. My lungs took in more air than they ever had in such a short period of time. Foul language usually put the taste of tar and bile on my tongue, but from him, it sent a line of heat from my knees to my lower back.

"I don't like that kind of talk." It was out of my mouth before I realized I didn't mean it.

"Maybe." He reached into his pocket and pulled out a white business card. "Maybe not."

I took the card. Antonio Spinelli, Esq., and a number in 213. I glanced up to ask him what kind of lawyer made douchebags lick puke off a car, but he was already walking toward a black Maserati. Bow Lips gently leaned Deirdre against the wall.

"Thanks," I said, pocketing the card.

"Take care of her." He indicated that I should sit next to Deirdre before one of the many smokers exiting the club did. "She's dangerous."

I smiled at him and watched as he got in the passenger side and they drove away. I sat next to my sister and waited for the ambulance.

Chapter 5.

I put the card in my pocket and rode in the ambulance with
Deirdre. My sister was chronically depressed, and she medicated
with alc ohol. We all knew the drill. She got wheeled in. People
shouted. They took her vitals. A nurse gave me scrubs so I could
get out of my puke-covered clothes. The V-neck top had wide
sleeves and teddy bears in a cloudy sky. My dressy heels were
absurd with the pink pants that were four sizes too big.

They gave Deirdre B vitamins, and once they'd determined
that she hadn't done any damage to her brain she couldn't afford,
they left me in the room with her. My stink-soaked clothes were
in a plastic bag under my chair. Before, I'd call Daniel. But
my new roommate and I had agreed that she'd be the person I
checked in with, since checking in was what I missed most.

—*I'm at the hospital with my sister.*
Everything ok. Won't be home.—

The text came immediately.

—**Breaking down the set in three
hours. Need me to come?**—

—*Sure. Sequoia*—

My jacket was crumpled in the plastic bag. I'd moved the lawyer's card to the pocket of the scrubs for reasons I couldn't articulate. It weighed forty pounds in my pocket. It had gotten warmer when the paramedics asked for my sister's stats, her insurance, her age, how many drinks she'd had. It vibrated and buzzed as I waited for her to regain consciousness.

—*Ok. Which sister?*—

—*Deirdre. She's been in sri lanka. You*
never met her.—

—*Boozy left-wing freedom fighter?*—

—*LOL yes*—

I went out to the ER waiting room. Sequoia was a nice hospital, but the next few hours were going on the "really bad times not interesting enough to even talk about" list. The waiting room was active late at night, but slower, as if the horrors of Los Angeles took a break for a few hours. Babies fussed, and the TVs screamed joyful network news. I went to the vending machine and stared at the library of packages, unable to decide what I didn't want the least.

A kid of about seven jostled me out of the way and jammed a dollar into the slot, punched buttons as if it was his job, and stood in front of me while the machine hummed. But nothing happened. No goodie was forthcoming.

I ran through the next day in my head. Katrina would have to drive me back to Frontage. I'd get my car, make it home, and—

There was a loud bang, as if a bullet had hit fiberglass, and I jumped, not realizing I'd spaced out. Antonio Spinelli, still in his black suit, touched the machine and, finding the spot he needed, banged again. Two bags of chips fell, and the kid jumped at them. The lawyer smirked at me and shrugged. He was more gorgeous in the dead, flat fluorescents than he'd been in the dark parking lot.

"You want something?" he asked.

He kept his eyes on my face, but I felt self-conscious about my scrub-clad body and dress shoes. "What are you doing here?" I sounded small and insignificant, probably because I was trying to speak while holding my breath.

He shrugged. "Getting you a late dinner." He indicated the array inside the machine like a tall blonde turning letters. "Cheese chips? Ring Pop?"

I felt alone on a Serengeti plain with a cheetah circling. "You waited for me all this time?"

"I noticed you might need a ride home, so I followed the ambulance."

"A lawyer. Chasing an ambulance."

He smirked, and I wasn't sure if he got the joke or if it was outside of his cultural matrix. "What kind of gentleman would I be?"

"Again. What are you doing here?" My mouth tasted as if a piece of week-old roast beef had been folded into it. I was wearing scrubs that wouldn't have fit even if they were the right size, and my spiked heels felt like torture devices. My head hurt, my sister was in the hospital for alcohol poisoning, and a beautiful god of a man wanted to share a Ring Pop with me.

Antonio took out a bill and fed the machine. "I think I made a bad impression in the parking lot." He punched more buttons than any one item required.

"Your intentions were good. Thank you for that."

"My methods, however?"

Things dropped into the opening. Chips, candy, crackers, cookies, *plop, plop, plop, plop.* He must have put a twenty in there.

"I'm trying not to think too hard about it."

"You were very composed." He crouched to retrieve his pile of packages. "I've never met a woman like that."

"Except for looking aroused?" I crossed my arms, feeling exposed.

"That, I've met." He handed me an apple, the one piece of real food available in the hospital vending machine. He looked at me in a way I didn't like. Not one bit.

Except I did like it. I took the apple. I became too aware of the teddy bears on my shirt and my hair falling all over the place. My lips were chapped, and my eyes were heavy from too many hours awake. Maybe that was for the best. Looking early-morning fresh would have made his gaze seem sexual rather than intense.

He stepped back next to an uncomfortable-looking plastic chair, indicating I should sit. Holding my apple to my chest, I sat. He dumped our meal into the seat next to me and sat on the other side of it.

"How's your sister?" he asked.

I sighed. "She'll be fine. I mean, she won't, because she'll do it again. But she'll be up and running by afternoon."

He looked pensive, plucking a bag of nuts from the chair and putting it back. "It's impossible to change what you are. You drink like that when you fight yourself."

"How did you get so educated on the matter?"

"I had an uncle."

He opened a granola bar, and I watched his finger slipping into the fold of cellophane, exerting enough pressure to weaken and split the bond between the layers. It took exactly no effort. A child could do it. But the grace of that simple thing was exquisite. I pressed my legs together because I kept imagining those hands flat on the insides of my thighs.

"It was my job to collect him in the mornings," he continued. "He supported my mother, so he had to go make money. Every morning, I had to look for him. I found him in the street, in the piazza, wherever. Passed out with wine all over his shirt. I splashed water on his face and sent him to work at the dock. I mean, he called me a *stronzo* first, but I got the job done."

His story opened doors and corridors to further questions. The possibility of spending hours in that waiting room with him was a little too appealing. I'd seen what he'd done to the man who'd kicked my sister, and I had the feeling he wasn't a normal lawyer. Something was up, and finding out was akin to stroking a snake to feel the click of the scales.

"What are you doing here?" I asked. "In Los Angeles?"

He shrugged. "The California bar is easy. And the weather's nice."

"My name is Theresa."

"I know." He smiled at my shocked expression, looking about as concerned as a cat on a windowsill. "I used to see you on TV during Daniel Brower's campaign for mayor. Part of it, at least. I think he might win."

I must have turned purple, though my face didn't shift and my shoulders stayed straight.

He cast his eyes down as if he'd said too much. "It's not my business, of course."

"It's Los Angeles's business, apparently, that my fiancé was having sex with his speechwriter. Any details in the paper you missed and want me to fill in?" I was having a complete emotional shut down. Not even his full lips or the arch of his eyebrows could pierce my veil of defensiveness. "That's why you were watching me at Frontage that first night. Trying to put the face with the story."

"No."

"I'm not interested in your pity, or in you proving yourself, or anything for that matter." I stood. I'd talked myself into a deep enough hole, and the shame of the entire incident swelled inside me. "Thanks for dinner."

I spun on my heel and walked to the nearest door that led outside. I should have headed back to Deirdre. I should have gone to the ladies' room. I should have gone to the desk. But outside looked so appealingly anonymous, as if I could walk into the darkness and disappear. Once I got there though, I had nowhere to go, and the cars speeding down LaCienega didn't slow enough for me to cross. In any case, I couldn't go far. Deirdre needed me.

I walked down the block as if I had a destination. I'd been foolish. I'd wanted him, spine to core, but he knew who I was. I couldn't run away from what had happened with Daniel. Everyone knew, and any relationship I had would be painted with the brush of my humiliation. I felt that beautiful hand on my elbow, and part of my body continued forward despite his best effort.

"Wait," he said, "you never let me finish."

"I don't want you to," I said, letting him hold my elbow while I caught my balance.

"I was watching you because yes, I wanted to place the face." I started to object, but he put his fingers to my lips and said, "And when I did, I was... how do you say?" He squinted as if trying to squeeze the word out of his brain. "Awestruck." I pulled away and he let go of me. "Don't go. It's not what you think. Yes, I saw you on TV with Brower. You always stood so straight, even when they attacked you. Reporters, the other side, even your own people. And you never cracked. Then tonight, you stand up and tell me to stop hurting that man, like it's your right under God to do it. You could run the world. Do you realize?"

I said nothing. I hated that he had observed my shame with Daniel so closely in such one-sided intimacy.

"Let me take you out," he said. "My attention isn't going to hurt you."

"Look, I'm sorry. You're nice enough. And I have to be honest, you're handsome. Very handsome." I couldn't look at him when I said that. "But I'm a curiosity to you. To me, it's still very real." I folded my arms so he had to release my elbow. A bus blew by us with a shattering roar, sending a warm breeze through our hair. "I'm just not ready."

"Let me take you out anyway."

"Tee Dray!"

I spun around. Katrina jogged toward me from the parking lot, carrying a huge satchel and wearing Uggs with her leggings. She was early, and not a minute too soon.

"I'm sorry," I said, backing away toward Katrina. "I can't." I felt her at my back, panting.

"Hi," she said.

I turned around and realized she wasn't saying hello to me. "Katrina, this is Antonio."

"*Ciao*," he said with a nod before he directed his gaze back at me. "You have my card, Contessa."

"I do."

"*Ciao* then." He smiled, nodded, and walked toward the parking lot entrance.

Katrina spun around to watch him as he turned and waved.

"Holy fucking hot fire."

"Yes. Holy hot fire."

"That's not the same guy, is it?" she asked.

"It is."

"Is he an actor? I could use him. Fuck, I could write feature films about the way he walks."

"Lawyer. Italian. Which is nice if you're into that sort of thing. You're early, by the way."

"We actually got shit done." We started back toward the hospital. "Michael was a bruiser. He asked about you," she said.

"Not interested."

"How's your sister?"

"Should be awake by now. Can you wait for me?"

"An hour. Then you drive yourself home," she said as if she meant it. She put her arm around my shoulder and walked me in.

Chapter 6.

"They'll send a priest if you want to see one," I said, sitting by Deirdre's bed.

"I don't need counseling." My sister looked flush and healthy and energetic, despite being waist-deep in sheets. Nothing like a mainline of B vitamins to bring a woman to the peak of health.

"They can't release you without it. And I'm sorry, but I agree with the policy. You could have died."

"I'm a grown woman." She threw off her sheets, exposing a blue hospital gown that matched my scrubs.

I put my hand on her shoulder. "Dee, please. I've got your vomit all over my clothes. We can get Dr. Weinstein back if you want."

She tucked one curly red lock behind her ear, where it would stay for three seconds before bouncing in front of her eyes again. "I want to go to work."

"You need a break from that job. It's turning you into a grouch."

"I can't do anything else," she said. "I don't know how."

One of the downsides of being incredibly wealthy was the ease with which one could go through life without marketable skills. The only ability she'd developed was compassion for people who didn't have what she had and contempt for those who did. Self-loathing went deep, a trademark Drazen trait.

"There's a trade school around the corner," I said. "You could learn to fix cars."

spin

"You think Daddy would buy me a shop in Beverly Hills?"

"Anything to get you out of social work. Heck, I'd buy you a shop."

She put her face in her hands. "I want to do God's work."

I held her wrists. "God didn't build you to see what you see every day. You're too sensitive."

She took her hands away from her face. "Can you go to that thing with Jon tonight? At the museum? I don't think I can take it."

Jonathan was only seen in public with his sisters in the hope of drawing back his ex-wife.

"If you give the counselor one hundred percent, I'll go."

She leaned back in the bed. "Fine."

"Thank you."

"You smell like a puke factory."

I kissed her head and put my arms around my crazy, delicate sister.

32.

Chapter 7.

Katrina was in the waiting room, sleeping on her binder and drooling on the breakdown script for the next day.

I sat by her head and put my hand on her shoulder. I felt guilty for calling her while she was in production, and I felt lonely for needing her so badly. "Come on, Directrix. I'm driving."

"Five minutes, Mom," she whispered.

By the time Katrina dropped me at Frontage, my little BMW was the only car in the lot, and condensation left a polka dot pattern on my windshield. It was a 1967 GT Cabrio with chrome detailing that wasn't happy about water drying on it. I shouldn't have bought it. The car was a death trap. But Daniel had gone to the automotive museum's auction to show his face, and I'd walked out with what he called LBT, the Little Blue Tink. He'd been annoyed, but I'd fallen in love.

I wasn't ready to end the night. Though the rising sun would end it for me, I wasn't ready to process it. It was almost six in the morning, and my brother never slept, so I called him.

"Hey, Jon," I said. "I saw your singer last night."

"I heard."

I could tell by his sotto voice and cryptic words that he wasn't alone. "You want the good news or the bad news?"

"Bad."

"Everything's fine, before you panic."

"Okay, I'm not panicked."

"Deirdre again."

"Ah," he said.

"And I didn't just pour her into bed. She had to be hospitalized. Nothing a few B vitamins couldn't fix, but honestly, I think she has a real problem. I saw her have two drinks, but she had a flask and she went to the bathroom, I don't know, fourteen times."

"You're exaggerating."

"Not by much. So I'm coming with you tonight."

"Fine."

"Can I be honest?" I didn't wait for his answer. "I think your perpetual availability isn't helping draw Jessica back."

"Very mature, Theresa. Very mature."

"Take a real woman, Jon. Stop being a patsy."

I never spoke like that to my brother or anyone. I rarely gave advice or told anyone to change, but I was tired, physically and emotionally. I hung up without saying good-bye. I had to get Katrina home and get ready for work.

Chapter 8.

I got to my office, where Pam waited for me. My assistant had neon pink hair in a 1940's style chignon, pierced nose and brow, and smart suit; a story of contradictions she called psychabilly. I hadn't heard of it before or since, but when her boyfriend showed up looking like Buddy Holly with tattoos, I got the aesthetic.

"You look wrung out," she said, as if wrung out was a compliment.

I'd cleaned up as much as I could, but make up could only achieve so much. "Thanks. I was sober for the whole thing. Did the late list come through?"

"It's printing. Arnie wants to see you," Pam said as she tapped on her keyboard. She chronically tapped out beats on the table and her knees.

"Did you get a new piercing?" I touched my forehead.

"Like it?" She waggled her brows and handed me a folder with the day's check reports. "Bobby got one on his... you know." She pointed downward.

I couldn't imagine what kind of face I made. Something broadcasting distaste and empathy, probably.

"It's hot," she whispered. "And for my pleasure."

"Grotesque, thank you."

"The DA's been calling you." Pam had started calling Daniel "The DA," since he was the district attorney, when we broke up. She said uttering his name made her sick, and though I told her I could fight my own battles, she'd never said his name again.

"What's he want?" I said around the lump in my throat.

"Lunch. I said you were busy."

"Set it up."

She looked at me over her rhinestone frames.

"I can handle it. Get us into the commissary," I said.

No one in the WDE commissary even bothered glancing at a mayoral candidate, or the mayor, or anyone for that matter. Everyone there worked in the business, so everyone had an important job. To approach someone in the commissary meant you didn't have access to them elsewhere. No one would admit they weren't cool enough to get a meeting with Brad Pitt. Too bad the food there tasted like cheap wedding fare.

"Your Monday three o'clock's been cancelled," Pam said.

"What? Frances?"

"Frances doesn't have the clearance to cancel a meeting for you." She pointed at a little double red flag on the time block. "Only Arnie's girl does."

I checked my watch. "I'm going to see him. Hold down the fort."

"Held. I'll set up the lunch."

I left her wrinkling her nose while she dialed Daniel's number.

***

In Los Angeles, windows separated the dogs from the bitches.

Not my saying. My sister Margie said it, and when I told Pam, she believed it so ardently she repeated it regularly. When I was moved to the only office in accounting with a window, she called me a newly minted dog.

Once.

"Oh, Ms. Drazen, you know it's a compliment."

"No one should ever repeat anything my sister says. She's out of her mind."

That one window, which took up only half the room—while all the other executives had full walls of Los Angeles behind them—could have meant the world to so many. To me, it didn't change a thing. I'd been born into four generations' worth of money. I had a job because I wanted one, which meant I could leave at any time. My value wasn't in my loyalty, but in my skill, which I'd take with me if I left.

The two walls of windows in Arnie Sanderson's office sat at right angles. Across from the north window was a twelve-foot-high mahogany shelving unit that housed antique tools of the agent's trade. Typewriter. Approval stamp. Cufflinks. Crystal decanter and glasses. Photos of agents gladhanding household names. The only things missing were a collection of super-white dental caps and rolled up hundred-dollar bills coated with cocaine residue.

"Theresa," he said when I came in. His jacket pulled at the gut, even though it was custom made, and his tie was held by a gold bar so out of style, it would be back in style in six months. "You all right?"

I assumed he was referring to the dark circles that screamed late night out. "Gene took some of us to see an act last night."

"Ah, Gene. I'm sure the bill will be of magnificent proportions. Sit." His smile, which sparkled from his white teeth to his eyes, was the product of decades of asking for things and getting them.

I sat on the leather couch. "It's nice to see you."

Actually, it wasn't. Being invited to his office meant something was wrong, especially in light of my three o'clock Monday meeting's cancellation.

"Can I get you something? Water? A drink? Hair of the dog?"

Only half the staff came in half sober on Fridays. It was the life. As if proving my unmade point, he poured himself a drink as amber as a pill bottle.

"I'm fine."

"I hear you're on Katrina's set. Michael's movie," he said.

Agents and producers called talent by their first name whether they'd ever pressed flesh with them or not. Arnie, of course, was one of the few who'd actually earned the right that everyone else took for granted.

"Script supervising in off hours. It's fun."

"I imagine you'd be good at continuity. And you picked the one director we represent who's a walking time bomb."

"She's my friend." I was suddenly, inexplicably, unusually nervous, as if he could see right through me.

He sat across from me and crossed his legs, an odd gesture for a man. "She's dangerous. She has entitlement issues. After that lawsuit with Overland, she's poison, to be honest. Be careful."

"Have you ever known me to be anything but careful?"

"You are famously vigilant." He smiled, but it was reserved. He really didn't want me working with Katrina; it was all over his face. "I wanted to thank you for getting so many of our clients off paper. Saves man hours and money. They love us for it."

"It's what you hired me to do."

"Everything's running so smoothly, I thought you might have a little time on your hands?"

"I still have to run the department," I said. "But if you had something in mind, I'm open to it."

"Well, it's irregular, if you will."

"I'm not much of a pole dancer."

He laughed gently. "Well, as that wasn't on your resume, I'm sure we can overlook it." He sipped his drink. "We rep a kid right out of USC. Matt Conway. You may have heard of him?"

"Oscar for best short last year."

"Nice kid. Shooting a little movie on the Apogee lot. They have some nice European sets over there. Mountains in the back, the whole thing."

"I've seen it," I said.

"He rented a dozen or so vintage cars. The little stupid boxy things with the long license plates. Well, the company that owns the cars has audit privileges, in case anything going wrong. It's irregular, like I said, but they're exercising the right, and they insisted the head of our accounting department do it. I thought they meant our internal accounting, but they meant you."

"Me?"

"Normally, I'd tell them to go pound sand, but this isn't some prop company. There are powerful people involved, and if I say no, the phone's going to start ringing."

"What am I looking for?"

"He'll tell you," he said.

"I have a department to run."

"Is that a no?"

"It's just a statement of fact."

"Good. We have a gentleman from the fleet rental and a representative from the studio coming at three, Monday."

Three o'clock. Of course. Arnie hadn't taken no for an answer in thirty years.

***

Daniel had been to the commissary before, on bank holidays when he had off and everyone in Hollywood worked. So when I got there, he was comfortably tapping on his phone, left alone for an hour during a tight campaign. Seeing him work the device tightened my chest. I'd thrown his last phone in the toilet.

"Hi," I said, sitting down and putting the linen napkin on my lap.

He pocketed his phone and smiled at me. "Thanks for seeing me."

I nodded, casting my eyes down. When would I stop playing the injured party? Why did I fall into victimhood so easily?

And why did he fall into the role of evildoer without so much as a blink? His hunched pose, something his handlers had trained out of him a year ago, returned. That lock of light hair, the one he used to brush away in a move the cameras hated, dropped in front of his forehead. I saw the effort he expended to not move it. I saw the extra tightness in his fingers as they wove together in front of him. I saw everything, and when I would have made an effort to relax him before, I just felt a thread of satisfaction.

I hated our dance. It made me sick. But I didn't know how to stop the music because I still loved him. The man who let me arrange the house any way I wanted, who laughed at my stupid jokes, who rubbed lube on me when I wasn't working right. The man who made such good but failed efforts to get me to orgasm with his fingers or his dick in me.

"How's Deirdre?" he asked then continued when I tilted my head. "One of the admins saw a Drazen admitted and called me. She thought it was you."

"Is that even legal?"

He shrugged. "I know people. It's my job. Is she okay or not?"

"She's fine."

I'd ordered our food ahead of time, and it came to our table in wide-rimmed white dishes that would go out of style at the turn of the next century.

"How have you been?" He shuffled his food around with the heavy silver fork. Because of his childhood impoverishment, he ate as quickly and cleanly as a steamshovel on amphetamines, so he only ate when his company was distracted by conversation.

"Fine, thank you. I'm script supervising for Katrina when I can, so I'm a little tired. But it's fun. She got Michael Greenwich for the lead, and he's been incredible. On the strength of his performance alone, she's hoping to get distribution."

He huffed. "I'm surprised anyone wants to deal with her after the lawsuit."

"Yes, she's just another uppity woman asking for what she's due."

"You know I don't mean it like that, Tink."

I stopped chewing. He wasn't supposed to call me that anymore. I looked out the window. "One day, we're going to get over this," I said, looking again at the man I loved. "Until then, let's avoid the small talk."

He cleared his throat. "The thing with us, it hurt me. My numbers. Especially on the east side, where they're really conservative."

"Yes, I know." God, the ice in my voice. It felt like someone else was talking. I could will myself quiet. I could will myself honest. But I couldn't will myself warm.

"I don't want you to think I'm just talking about what happened like it's all about me and the campaign, okay? But that's the business of the lunch. If you want to talk about it on a more personal level, I'm happy to."

"You're fine. I get it. Go on."

"I have a Catholic Charities thing Thursday," he said.

"Okay."

"They're supporting me because I'm not sitting still on income inequality, but the thing with us—"

"And Clarice."

"And Clarice—who is gone—was a sticking point. They almost pulled out. So I'm here to ask for a symbolic gesture from you."

"Of?" I asked, but I knew what it was.

"Of forgiveness. Christian forgiveness that'll play with the San Gabriel Valley. Your family is a big diocesan donor. It won't go unnoticed."

"What does this symbolic gesture of Christian forgiveness entail?"

"If you could attend the fundraiser and stand by me." He held up his hand as if warding off an objection I hadn't yet made. "Not as my fiancée, obviously, but as a supporter. As someone whose priorities are my own."

I chewed. Swallowed. Sipped water. I knew I'd agree, but I didn't want to throw myself at his feet. He didn't deserve it. Or I didn't.

I'd heard a lot about what Daniel deserved. I'd heard that he was a worthless scumbag, and I'd heard promises to make his life in the mayor's mansion a living hell. Those promises meant nothing to me. No one would hurt Daniel over infidelity. In five years, it would be forgotten. So I'd kept my venom to myself in public, and I released it around my family and Katrina.

But something came into my mind—a vision of Antonio beating Daniel's head against a car. I smelled the blood and heard the crack of his nose as it broke from the impact. I imagined a tooth clacking across the metal, his contorted face as he said he was sorry, and Antonio and I partnering over the difference between his regret and his remorse.

"Why are you smiling?" he asked.

I changed the subject. "We decided the public appearances weren't working."

"And normally, I'd think it would just remind everyone of my weakness. But in this case, if people see you forgiving, they might follow. I can't win unless I do something."

I leaned back, appetite gone. "I can see the op ed pieces now. Another political wife forgives her overambitious man's failings with other women. Judge her. Don't judge her. She's a feminist. She's the anti-feminist. She's a symbol for all of us. None of that falls on you. It's all on me."

"I know."

"You are so lucky I don't want Bruce Drummond in office."

The air went out of him. He didn't move, but I saw the slight shift of his shoulders and the release of tension in his jaw. "I can't thank you enough."

"We'll figure something out."

"I'd still marry you if you'd have me back."

"Daniel, really—"

He leaned forward as if propelled. "Hear me out. Not as the maybe mayor. As me. Dan. The guy you taught how to walk straight. The guy who bit his nails. That guy's going to be seventy years old one day, and he's going to regret what he did. I want you back. After this campaign, win or lose, let me love you again."

Joy, terror, shock, sadness all fought for my next words. None of them won the race to get from my brain to my mouth.

"I swore I wouldn't do what I just did," he said. "But I miss you. I can't hold it in anymore."

My words came out with no emotion in them. "I'm not ready."

"I'll wait for you, Tink. I'll wait forever."

I didn't respond because I couldn't imagine myself being ready, and I couldn't imagine committing myself to anyone else.

Chapter 9.

On Monday, I had twenty minutes before my meeting with the fleet guy and the studio rep, exactly enough time to get briefed by Pam.

"Studio's sending a courier," she said, leaning into the screen. "They said you could handle it."

"Wow," I interjected, "they don't even pretend to care."

Pam dropped her voice to nearly inaudible. "Rumor is Matt got the cash for his short from a Hollywood loan shark, and Overland covered the note to the tune of way too much. So if there's a bus coming, he might get thrown under it."

"They need to get their own accountants to do their dirty work. They have the best of the best."

She slipped her rhinestone horn-rimmed glasses halfway down her nose and looked at me over them. "What do you think you are?"

"Adequate, since you asked."

She shook her head and went back to work. I cleared my desk of a few million in incidentals before going to the conference room to do Arnie his favor.

***

The conference room was huge, set into the office's bottom floor. Two sides were glass, looking over the reception area, and the other two walls were glass, looking out onto Wilshire

Boulevard. It was designed for big faces to be seen together by the rest of the agency and by whomever was waiting in reception. Appointments might be based around making sure Mr. Twenty-Million-Dollar-A-Picture Actor was seen shaking hands with Mr. Academy-Award-Winning-Director in front of Ms. Top-Agent just as Ms. Actress-Who-Refused-The-Nude-Scene waited for an appointment. Like everything in the entertainment industry, it was maximum drama, maximum visibility.

Every time I went into that particular conference room, I checked the smoothness of my stockings, the lay of my hair, the seams between my teeth, even when I was just meeting a messenger to pass over audit materials. What used to arrive in a banker's box of paper and ledgers and folders now came in the form of a flash drive and a manila envelope with a few summary sheets, which were useless. They were delivered by a short man in shorts, sneakers, and a flat cap. Matt's line producer.

"I'm Ed, nice to meet you," he said as he shook my hand and slid the hard drive and envelope onto the table.

"Nice to meet you too. What do we have here?"

"Everything up to the minute for the whole production. Hope you can help with this. It was kind of unexpected."

I was about to respond and open the summary schedules so I could ask intelligent questions. Then I was going to finish my work and pick up dinner. I was feeling a turkey sandwich, salad, and bottle of water.

But that got shot out the window in a storm of hormone shrapnel when I saw Arnie coming through reception with a man in a dark suit named Antonio Spinelli. They were talking, but through the window, I saw Antonio's eyes flick up at me and a smile stretch across his face. I frowned when Arnie opened the door to the conference room.

"Ms. Drazen," he said cheerfully, "how is the handoff going?"

I slid the papers from the envelope just to distract myself, but my hands shook with rage or nerves. Possibly both.

"Just got here," said Ed.

"This is Mr. Spinelli," Arnie said in full agent-smarm. "He rents exotic cars to the business."

"I know," I said, cutting off my boss in a way I never would. I immediately caught my faux pas and held out my hand. "We've met."

"Ms. Drazen." He took my hand, and I felt tingling heat between my legs. "I wanted to say hello before you started."

"Hello," I said flatly, releasing his hand but not his gaze, which seemed just as physical.

"Great," Arnie said. "I'm heading into a meeting." He shook Ed's hand, nodded to Antonio, and left.

When the glass door clicked behind him, I spoke. "We've got it from here, Ed." I shot him a look. We were on the same side. I was watching out for him.

As if he understood, he nodded. "Later." Ed tipped his cap and left.

Only the pull of the air between Antonio and me remained.

"This is flattering," I said, "but it's not going to work."

"You can't prove they didn't take care of the cars?"

"Oh, you name it, I can prove it."

"Good, I wanted the best."

"You got me instead, but that doesn't mean you've got me."

"So you say."

I tried not to smile. That would only encourage him. The last thing the arrogant ass needed was encouragement. "I won't deny I'm attracted to you. I'm sure I'm not the first. But I'm not a conquest. I don't like being chased, especially not through the offices of WDE. This is my job, Mr. Spinelli, not a mousehole. You can't stick your paw in and hope to catch me. I don't care to mix business with displeasure. Now if you'll excuse me."

I reached for the flash drive and envelope, and he stood in my way, getting close enough for me to catch the forested smell of his cologne.

"I could kiss you right now," he said.

"You wouldn't dare."

The windows suddenly felt like cameras. I felt the presence of everyone's eyes as if they were pressure on my skin.

"I will. And you might push me away, but not before you kiss me back. You know it. I know it. And everyone else in this office is going to know it," he said.

"Don't."

"See me then. Let me take you out Thursday night."

I was relieved. That was the perfect out. "I have plans on Thursday."

"Cancel them."

"I can't. It's a fundraiser."

"Catholic Charities?" He raised an eyebrow. If it was at all possible for him to look sexier, he did.

"Yes." I stood straight. I didn't want to have to explain it, but I had a compulsion to excuse myself I had to quell.

"Good." He stood straight. "I was invited to that. We'll go together."

"No!"

"So we should see each other another time, then?"

Of course not. We should be together some other never. But I hesitated, and that was my mistake.

"I think I should see you before the fundraiser," he said, "because I want to go with you and show Daniel Brower what he's missing."

"You going to take him out to the parking lot and beat him up for me?"

"He deserves far worse."

Knowing better than to encourage him, I held up my chin. "I'll decide what he deserves. Thank you, though."

"Good. I'll pick you up Wednesday at eight."

"I'm busy."

"I'll have to kiss you now then." He stepped forward.

I swallowed because his lips, a step closer to mine, were full and satiny, and more than anything, my mouth wanted to feel them.

"Follow me please," I said like an automaton.

I brushed past him without waiting for a response, walking out the door and down the hall with the manila envelope in my arm. I nodded to my associates and knew he was behind me from the sense of movement and heat at my back. I slipped into a windowless, empty conference room and closed the door when he entered.

"Mister Spinelli—"

On the way to the closed office, I'd prepared a short speech about respecting my boundaries, but I swallowed every word when those satin lips fell on mine. His kiss was a study in paying attention, reacting to me as I reacted to him with increasing intensity. When his tongue touched mine, I lost myself in desire. His hands stayed on my neck, and I became aware of their power and gentleness.

When I put my hands on him, he moved closer, and with a brush on my thigh, I felt his erection. Oh, to be anywhere else. To explore that rigid dick, to feel it in me while those lips hovered over mine. My legs could barely hold me up when he kissed my neck.

"Wednesday," he whispered, the warmth of his breath and timbre of his voice as arousing as the touch of his lips.

"You don't really care about the cars."

"No, I don't."

"I'm not making it up. I told my friend I'd be on her set after work Wednesday. I can't ditch her. Friday. We can do Friday."

"I accept the spirit of your agreement."

He reached behind me and turned the doorknob. I put my hair in place and thought cold thoughts. He left, and I watched him stride down the carpeted hall. I didn't move until he was out the office door. I couldn't believe he left it like that, without setting up a definite time and place for me to be flat on my back. I felt ill at ease as I scooped up the audit materials and headed back to my little window in my little office in my little corner of the Hollywood system.

Chapter 10.

"You want to fuck her."

Michael nodded. He and Katrina sat on stools at the counter of a tiny coffee shop she'd rented for the scene with staff all around. I held my clipboard and waited, having been told to stay within Michael's eyesight.

"Right," he said.

"You know if you fuck her once, she's yours."

This conversation happened as if no one was around. As if there weren't three gaffers playing with the lights and keys with clothes hangers clipping wires and aligning scrims. As if the assistant camera person wasn't holding up his little light meter to every color of everything and calling out numbers.

"You have to fuck her," Katrina said with real urgency. "You're not getting it."

"I'm getting it."

Katrina hauled off and slapped Michael in the face. The sound echoed in the halls and rooms of my brain. I flinched and looked at them. I wasn't supposed to. That was very personal actor/director business, and everyone else had the good sense to ignore it.

Michael made eye contact with me as it happened.

"That," she said. "That feeling. Right now."

"I have it," he said, putting his hand to his lips as if he wanted to hide his face.

"Good. Get to makeup." She winked at me as Michael strode off, then she called to the cameraman, "We're shooting him from the right. Have the stand in mark it." She walked off, barking more orders, and I marked the change in angle on my clipboard.

We would be filming late, and I girded myself with coffee and the knowledge that helping Katrina, even in the tiny role as part-time script supervisor, would right a great wrong that had been done her.

Michael played the scene, which did not include the woman in question, but her best friend. His character was about to bed her out of spite, like a man on a mission to save his testicles. He was riveting. He seized the scene, the set, the crew, and the mousy character who had no idea what she was getting embroiled in. He put his hands up her skirt as if he owned what was under it, but his character didn't take an ounce of responsibility for what he was doing.

"Cut!" shouted Katrina.

I noted the shot and take, but only after the scene was fully broken. "There's your Oscar," I mumbled to Katrina.

"I just want someone to touch this thing with a ten-footer." She took my clipboard and flipped through the pages on it. "We never got that last line on page thirty. I think we can ADR it."

"I think WDE will get behind you. Honestly. As long as you promise not to sue anyone again."

She made a *pfft* sound that promised nothing. "Dinner break, everyone!"

A production assistant ran up to me as I tucked my papers away. "There's a man here asking for you."

It took me about half a second to figure out who he was. "Dark hair and brown eyes?"

"Yeah. He brought dinner."

"Of course he brought me dinner." I had to process that while fixing my hair and straightening my sleeves.

"No," he said. "He brought *everyone* dinner. He brought *you* wine."

***

Movie sets that weren't dependent on sunlight stayed up all day. So though I'd shown up at six p.m. to relieve the other script supervisor, the set had already been up for twelve hours. Because no one left when there was work to be done, meals and snacks were provided to the entire crew. Bigger productions got more services, with above the line crew (actors, director, producers) getting gourmet catering, and below the line crew (camera, grips, gaffe, PA, AD, on and on and on) getting something good but less noteworthy. On Katrina's set, everyone got the same mediocre food from a truck wedged into the corner of the parking lot. A few long tables with folding chairs took up parking spaces. The day Antonio showed up for dinner, our French fry and burger habit was broken.

He had a bottle of red wine tucked under his arm and wore a grey sports coat with blood red polo. A woman in her sixties stood under his arm as he talked to Katrina. In front of them were four chafing dishes, plates, utensils, and a line of people.

"You do not get to invade my set," Katrina said, but I saw her eye the food ravenously. It was peasant food—meaty, saucy deliciousness that would satiate everyone for another four or five hours.

"*Mea culpa*," he said. "Your script supervisor accepted a dinner invitation, and Zia Giovana thought it would be rude to bring only for us."

"It's my fault," I said. "I forgot to tell you."

She spun and gave a smirk just for me. "You lie."

"If it means you can just eat, I'm guilty as charged." I pointed at Antonio. "You, sir, are pushy."

"As charged," he said. "Let me make it up to you."

"I think you just did." A plate of lasagna was pushed into my hands, but Antonio took it from me and passed it to the person behind me.

"Come on. I'm not feeding you outside a trailer."

He pulled me, but I yanked back. "I have to work."

Katrina didn't even look up from her food. "We have to set up the next shot. I'll text you when I need you. Get out of here."

I let Antonio put his arm around me and lead me onto the sidewalk. He held the wine bottle by the neck with his free hand. The neighborhood was light-industrial hip, with factories being converted into lofts and warehouses housing upscale restaurants.

"There's a place around the corner," he said. "No liquor license yet, so you bring your own."

"Let me see." I held my hand out for the bottle and inspected the label. "Napa? You brought a California wine?"

"It's not good?"

"It's a great wine, but I figured, you know, Italian?"

He laughed. "I was trying to not be pushy. Meet you halfway."

"This is how you say 'not pushy'?"

"You can run. I won't chase you."

"You won't?" I handed him the bottle.

He smiled. "Yeah. I will."

"Has it occurred to you that the chasing might be what you like about me, and that if I stop running, you might get bored?"

"I don't get bored. There's too much to do."

"It's funny," I said. "That's kind of what I find most boring. Everything to do."

"You're doing the wrong things, no? What do you love?"

We crossed onto a block of restaurants. The cobblestone streets were crowded. Tables were set on the sidewalks. Heat lamps kept the chill at bay.

"I don't love anything, really."

"Come on. The last thing you enjoyed, that made you feel alive."

I stopped walking, feeling disproportional frustration with his questions.

He turned to face me and walk backward. "Kissing me doesn't count."

"Funny guy."

A parking valet in a white shirt and black bowtie nearly ran into me, dodged, and opened a car door.

"Think hard," Antonio said. "The last thing that made you love life."

"Saying it would be inappropriate."

He raised an eyebrow. "I could learn to love this thing too, I think."

My annoyance turned into cruelty. "The last thing I loved doing? Working with Daniel on his campaign. I miss it."

Still walking backward, arms out to express complete surrender, he said, "Then, to make you happy, I announce that I will run for mayor."

I laughed. I couldn't help it. He laughed with me, and I noticed how reserved it was for a man who claimed to enjoy life.

He was on me before I could take in another second of his smile. He pushed his mouth on mine, his arms enveloping me, his hands in my hair. My world revolved around the sensations of him, his powerful body and sweet tongue, his crisp smell, the scratch of the scruff on his chin, and the way he paid attention to his kiss.

I matched his attention so carefully that when we got knocked into by a valet, I gasped. Antonio pulled me close, holding me up and protecting me at the same time.

The valet held up his hands. "I'm so sorry." He backed away toward a waiting car, reaching for the handle.

"You're sorry?" Antonio asked. "You don't look sorry."

I'd be the first to admit he didn't look sorry. He looked interested in opening the car door.

"It's okay, Antonio. He didn't do it on purpose."

He looked down at me for a second before looking back at the valet. "He could have knocked you over."

"But he didn't."

The valet opened the door with one hand and with the other, in a slight movement that could be denied later, flicked his hand, as if dismissing Antonio. Quick as a predator, Antonio took two steps toward the valet and pushed him against the car. I stepped into the street, heel bending on the cobblestone, and got between them. The valet's face was awash in fear, and Antonio's had an intensity that scared me.

"Antonio. Let's go, before I have to go back to work," I said.

He held his finger up to the valet's face. "You're going to be careful. Right?"

"Yeah, yeah." The man looked as though he wanted to be anywhere else.

He stepped back, and I put my hand on his arm. He looked at me with an unexpected tenderness, as if grateful I'd pulled him from oncoming traffic.

"Is there a problem here?"

The authoritative voice cut our moment short. Antonio and I looked to its source.

A short man in a zip-up black jacket and black tie, with a moustache and comb-over, appeared to recognize Antonio when we turned toward him. "Spin."

"Vito." Antonio looked the man up and down, pausing on his tag for *Veetah Valet Service – Proprietor.* He touched it. "Really?"

"I can explain."

"Yes, you can. After I bring the lady to our table. You'll be here."

"Yes, boss."

Antonio put his arm around me and walked toward an Italian restaurant with tables outside.

"What was that about?" I asked.

"He works for me. I'm going to have to talk to him for a minute."

"It wasn't a big deal about the valet."

"It's not about the valet."

I dropped my arm from his waist. He'd closed himself off so suddenly that touching him seemed out of place.

A young man with menus approached. "Outside or inside?"

"In," Antonio answered, giving the waiter his bottle.

He brought us to a table inside. Antonio held my chair for me and sat across the table, looking a million miles away.

"What happened?" I asked. "You look really annoyed."

He took my hand. "Trust me, it's not you."

"I know it's not me. What did that guy do?"

"He's not supposed to run other businesses while he works for me. That's the rule."

"That's a weird rule."

He smiled but looked distracted. "Let me go talk to him. Then you'll have my full attention."

I tapped my watch. "Quickly. I could turn into a pumpkin at any moment."

After Antonio walked away, the waiter returned with two glasses and our bottle of Napa wine. He poured a touch in my glass, made small talk, filled both glasses, and left.

I waited dutifully, tapping on my phone and watching people. I was walking distance from home and a few blocks from the set, but I wanted to be at that table. I was hungry, and I liked the Antonio I'd walked there with.

The wall facing the street was all windows. Past the rows of outdoor tables, I saw the lights change and cars roll by. Valets ran back and forth with keys and tickets. Antonio came into view, pinching a cigarette to his mouth and letting the smoke drift from out casually. What a stunning man he was. Maybe not in the same affable mood as he had been on the walk to the restaurant, but the intensity that condensed around him made me unable to look away.

He took a last drag and flicked his cigarette into the street. Then he walked in, smoke still drifting from his mouth. "Sorry about that," he said when he sat.

"Everything okay?"

"Yeah. Just a little talk."

The waiter came, we heard the specials, and ordered.

Antonio picked up his wine. "*Salute.*"

I held up my glass and looked at his when they clinked. His hand was firm and powerful, all muscle and vein, and his knuckles were scraped raw. I brushed the backs of my fingers against them.

"Antonio? Were you just talking? Or do they drag when you walk?"

He smiled. He'd gone out tense and returned relaxed. "One of the valets pushed me into a wall. I tried to break my fall, and this is what happened. These guys, they're paid per car, so they all jump to open doors a little too quick. How is the wine?" His smile was deadly.

"Good. What part of Italy are you from?"

"Napoli. The armpit of Italy, my mother used to say."

"And you came here for the weather and the easy access to litigator privileges?"

He smirked. "Do I have to answer everything right away?"

"Chasing me around won't go well if you don't."

He leaned over and touched my upper lip. Having him that close, I wanted to let those fingers explore my body. "You tell me where you got this scar. Then I'll tell you why I came here."

"I got the scar from a boy."

"Ah. And I came here because of a girl."

Appetizers came, filling little dumplings drenched in red sauce. He slipped a couple on my plate then a couple on his.

"You followed a woman here?" I watched him eat with clean efficiency.

"I followed men." He moved on to the next subject as if his life wasn't worth lingering on, brushing it off with a practiced, charming facility. "And this boy? His cutting wit, perhaps?"

"His high school ring. This girl. Was she chasing you?" I looked at him over my wine glass.

"No. She's back home."

"The girl is home, and you chased a man here because of her?"

"Close enough. What happened to the boy?" he asked.

"He's dead."

"Note to self. Don't scar Theresa Drazen."

I raised my wine glass to my lips to hide my expression. He'd gotten closer to a truth than he realized.

"So you own a hell of a lot of cars, a restaurant, and you're a lawyer," I said. "You contribute enough to the charity of your choice to get invited to the fundraisers. Oh, and you don't like Porsches. You can beat a guy nearly unconscious with your bare hands. You're a very interesting guy, Mister Spinelli."

He touched my hand with the tips of his fingers, finding a curve and tracing it. "Running an accounting department for the biggest agency in Hollywood. Working on the mayoral candidate's campaign. Helping your friend with her movie in your spare time. And the most poised, graceful woman I ever met. I'm not half as interesting as you."

I formulated an answer, maybe something clever or maybe I'd continue to ask uncomfortable questions, but my phone dinged. It was Katrina's new AD.

—*We're starting in ten*—

"This has been fun," I said. "I have to go."

He stood, reaching into his pocket. "I'll walk you."

He tossed a few twenties down and went to the door with me, putting his hand on my back as we exited. I pressed my lips together, avoiding a silly smile. I liked his hand there.

I didn't see Vito around. The valets were still working the block quickly, if less exuberantly.

"Tell me something," I said. "Why weren't you afraid that someone would call the cops that night with the Porsche? I mean, if you didn't break that guy's nose, I'll eat my shoe."

"Tell me what you think. Why would that be the case?" He put his hands in his pockets as he walked.

"That's a common debate team switch. Putting the speculation on me."

"Speculate." He smiled like a movie star, and I couldn't help but smile back.

"I'd rather you told me."

"Maybe I've met enough cops in my profession to know how to talk to them, should it come to that."

"Which profession is that?"

"I'm a lawyer."

I hadn't thought much of our harmless back and forth, but when he reminded me he was a lawyer, I caught a tightness in his voice. He glanced away. Most people were puzzles one had to simply collect enough pieces to figure out. My questioning had merely been fact-harvesting until he subtly evaded something so simple.

"If I look up criminal cases you've filed, what would I find? I mean, cases where you've dealt with the LAPD."

He looked down at the curb as we crossed the street, holding me back when a car came even though I'd stopped. "I'm a lawyer for my business. I've only had a couple of clients, and mostly they need my help talking to the police. Anything else you feel like you need to know?" He said it with good humor, but there was a wariness to his tone.

"Yes." We got to the outer edge of the set, where the street was closed off to keep it silent.

"What?"

I knew I shouldn't ask, but I was tired and still hungry, and the wine had sanded away my barriers. "Is Vito still outside the restaurant running his business?"

The look on his face melted me, as if a fissure had opened and he was trying desperately to keep the lava from pouring out. Then he smiled as if just having decided to let it all go. "Contessa, you are trouble."

"Is that good or bad?"

"Both."

My phone dinged again. I didn't look at it. I knew what it was about. "I have to go."

"*Come vuoi tu.*" He cupped my cheek in his hand and kissed me quickly before walking away, the picture of masculine grace. He didn't look back.

Chapter 11.

I strapped up my stockings with the TV on. I saw it behind me in the mirror. Daniel wore his pale grey suit and tie, ice in the sun. He'd done well at the debate that afternoon, keeping himself poised, still, and focused. He was the perfect Future Mister Mayor.

BRUCE DRUMMOND: My opponent hasn't opened a serious case against any crime organization in over a year. Just because it's peacetime, do we sit on our laurels?

I hadn't heard from Antonio since he'd left me at the set. I'd been tempted to reach out to him, but to what end? As I watched Daniel, I knew I still had feelings for him. How could I get involved with someone else? How could I take Daniel back? How could I use another man to break my holding pattern?

DANIEL BROWER: Believe me, my office has been gathering information and evidence against a number of organizations. We won't open a case unless we're sure we have the evidence we need. Please, let the people know if your administration will recklessly accuse citizens, so they can start looking for an independent prosecutor.

Antonio would be at the fundraiser. Though I was excited to see him, despite the fact that I had to avoid him, he'd become tight and unreadable. He'd avoided telling me about his business, and his story about being pushed by a valet was absurd. Vito hadn't gone home whistling Dixie. Antonio was Italian. From Naples. Was he a lawyer or criminal? Or both?

BRUCE DRUMMOND: In closing, I love my wife. She's the only woman for me, and that's why I married her. As your mayor, I'd never distract—

I liked nice men. Lawful men. Men with a future, a career, who could safely support children. I wasn't the type to look for the dangerous, exciting guys.

The dress went over my head in one movement. I twisted, struggled, and got the zipper up by myself.

***

It was eighty degrees and humid as hell, the wettest, nastiest, buggiest fall in L.A. history. Totally unexpected. Nothing anyone from the Catholic Charitable Trust could have foreseen when they'd planned an outdoor event ten months before. A string quartet played in the background, and wait staff carried silver trays of endive crab and champagne flutes. I made my way through the crowd alone, smiling and sharing air kisses. The house was a Hancock Park Tudor, kept and restored to the standards of a hotel as if the taste had been wrapped, boxed, and shipped in from a decorator's mind.

I was standing by the pool with Ute Yanix, talking about Species—the only raw foods place in L.A. that served meat—when Daniel crept up behind me. Ute's eyes lit up like a Christmas tree, and she brushed back her long straight hair like a silk curtain. Daniel did have a certain something. That thing had made him a frontrunner before the race even started.

"Ute, I'm glad you could make it," he said.

"You know I support you. All Hollywood does, whether we say it in public or not."

"I appreciate you being here publicly then." His hand found mine. "It's even more important than the donation."

She laughed a few decibels louder than necessary. "Now more than ever, huh?"

And with a look at me, the heiress in the candidate's corner, she implied the ugliest things. The first and most dangerous was that Daniel had been running the campaign on my money and now couldn't.

"I assure you, donations have always been appreciated." My smile could have lit the Hollywood sign.

The sexting incident was never mentioned on the fundraising floor, but in the bathroom, whispered voices, offered words of support, empathy, understanding, and others were clearly derisive. I had stopped fielding both sentiments.

I didn't hear the rest of the conversation. Over Ute's shoulder, I saw a man in a dark suit. Lots of men in dark suits milled around, but they had jeans, open collars, ties optional. He wore a suit like a woman wore lingerie, to accentuate the sexual. To highlight the slopes and lines. To give masculinity a definition. He held his wine glass to me, tearing my clothes off and running his hands over my skin from across the room.

"...but what you're going to do about the traffic—"

"I'll be Mayor, not God." They both laughed.

I'd lost most of the conversation during my locked gaze with Antonio Spinelli. "Excuse me," I said to my ex and the actress. "Duty calls."

I walked into the house. The unwritten rule was if the party was in the backyard, guests stayed in the backyard. Wandering off into the personal spaces was bad manners, but I couldn't help it. I went to the back of the kitchen, to a back hall with a wool Persian carpet and mahogany doors.

"Contessa."

I didn't have a second to answer before he put his hands on my cheeks and his mouth on mine. I didn't move. I didn't kiss him back. I just took in his scent of dew-soaked pine, wet earth, and smoldering fires. He pulled back, unkissed but not unwanted, his hands still cupping my face.

He brushed his thumb over my lower lip, just grazing the moist part inside. "I want you. I haven't stopped thinking about you."

"What happened then?" All my resolve to not use him as a rebound went out the window. "You froze me out yesterday."

"I don't like answering questions about myself."

"I can't be with you if I don't know you."

"Do you want me?"

His breath made patterns on my face. I could have pushed him away, but his attention was an angle, a point of reference, and I was but a line defined by it.

"Yes," I whispered, putting my head against the wall.

"Let's have each other then. My body and your body. No expectations. No questions."

Before I could get offended, he kissed me hard, hurting me. His tongue probed my lips, my teeth, pushing my head against the wall. I was aware of every inch of his body, its warmth, its supple curves, the hair on his face, and I yielded. My insides melted, pooling between my legs. I moved with him like a wave, tongues dancing, jaws aligning. I fell into that kiss, its taste of wine and sweet water, the hum vibrating from the back of his throat. I thought I would burst from my hips outward.

He pulled away with a gasp, still close to me, his eyes darting across my features. "You're blushing. And you're panting, just a little."

I couldn't speak. I wanted him to kiss me again. My body wanted it. The hairs on my arms stood up when I thought about it.

He put his hand to my chest, between my breasts, and pressed a little. "Your heart is beating hard. This is what it takes."

He moved his hand slightly, brushing my hard nipple through my dress. I wanted him to stop, but I didn't want it to end. If I spoke, the spell would be broken. I'd have to go back to the other me, that spurned, unwanted woman. I opened my mouth but just shook my head. What had I become? What was wrong with me?

"Since the minute I saw you," he said into my neck, "I've wanted to open your legs and take you."

His words had fingers, and as he spoke, they drifted down my body, fondling me and arousing me. No one had ever spoken like that to me, because I would have laughed with discomfort. But when Antonio said it, I forgot everything but his voice and the image of him moving over me.

"I'm not good at casual sex," I said in a breath.

"I never said it would be casual."

I didn't know what he meant. I didn't know how sex could be just two bodies meeting without being classified as meaningless. I couldn't wrap my head around it because he was near me, his hands on my hips, the scruff of his face brushing my neck.

"Take me," I said before I thought about it.

Like a cat leaping into action, he pulled me through an ajar door, clicking it behind us. We were in a bathroom with marble tiles and double sinks. White curtains. A thousand details I couldn't absorb because his lips were on mine.

When I heard him lock the door, I surrendered to what was happening. I stopped worrying about where I was or what the future might bring. I tangled my hands in his hair and kissed him for all I was worth. He pulled my knee up over his hip, stroking the back of my thigh. I tried to remember to breathe, but when he leaned into me and I felt the hardness between his legs against the softness between mine, I forgot.

"I'm going to fuck you right here," he growled. "Are you ready?"

"Yes." The word came out in a hiss.

"Yes, what?" He pushed against me. "What do you want me to do to you?" He took my hands from his hair and put them above me, pinning me to the wall as he kissed my neck.

"Fuck me." I said it so softly a butterfly wouldn't have heard me.

"Say it again. But this time, own it."

"Fuck me." A little louder.

He let go of my hands. His fingers brushed past my breasts to my waist, where they pushed me down against his erection.

"You are so sweet," he whispered, wrapping my other knee around him, pinning me with his hips. "*Dolce.* The way you don't like to say the word fuck, and you say it to me anyway. I know how bad you want me to make you come."

With that, he hitched me up and carried me to the vanity. He balanced me on it as he kissed me, grinding between my legs and driving me crazy. I yanked up my skirt.

"Antonio," I said, "protection."

"I have it."

I spent a little time worrying about having sex with a man who carried condoms around. Just a second. Just a stab of my real self, the one who was going to walk out of that bathroom when we were done. He took half a step back and pulled my knees apart. I leaned back as he slipped his fingers under my garter belt, finding the crotch of my panties.

"I like these," he said.

"Thank you."

He poked his finger through the lace and yanked with his other hand. The lace gave way with a bark of a rip, leaving my underwear with a gaping hole. He stroked me. I didn't know if I'd ever been that wet.

"I can't help it. I have to taste you." He put his face at the inside of my thigh and brushed his tongue on the sensitive skin. His hands stroked, tongue flicking, lips a soft center to the roughness of his face. When he made it to my pussy with a soft suck at my clit, I moaned. "Do you like it?" he asked before he circled my opening with his tongue.

"Yes."

"Yes what?"

"Yes, suck it. Eat me. Take me with your mouth."

The string quartet purred outside, and the party hummed along while I begged for a man's tongue on me. His tongue flicked, finding every want, every emptiness, and filling it with sensation. He sucked just a little then ran the flat of his tongue over my clit until my pussy felt like a bursting balloon.

"Antonio." My voice squeaked. I was on the edge.

"Come," he said, looking up at me. "I'm still going to fuck you."

When he put his lips on me again, his eyes watching me over the horizon of my gathered skirt, I let him fill me. I came hard, lifting my hips as he grabbed my thighs to keep me from falling over. I was beyond cries, beyond words. I was just a receptacle for the pleasure of a tiny percentage of my body.

I didn't have a second to breathe before he positioned himself above me. His pants were open, and his dick lay against my engorged clit. I reached down. He'd gotten it out and wrapped while he was eating me.

"You're very skilled," I said. "And you're huge."

He put his fingers in me. I was sensitive and swollen, soaked in desire.

"You're tight. So tight. Fuck." His eyes went to half-mast, and he sucked in a breath. "Spread your legs all the way."

I did, and he guided the head of his dick into me. I stretched when he thrust, a little sting of pain drowned by pleasure.

"You okay?" he asked.

I nodded. I felt as if I had a telephone pole in me, but I wouldn't complain about it. Maybe I should have asked him to go slow, because he shoved himself in until my expression told him he couldn't go any farther. He shifted my hips then pushed forward. He found space to fill and drove into me up to the base, pushing his body into me. I put my hands on his face, and he leaned down. We were eye to eye, nose to nose, bodies moving together, the swell of tension returning.

"You're beautiful," I said, my thumb on his lips.

He kissed my thumb, running his tongue along the length as he fucked me. We were dressed up but joined in our most vulnerable places. My back hurt where it was pushed against the stone vanity, and my shoulder was jammed into a cabinet. I heard the sounds of the party, and one of my shoes was about to fall off. I felt ripped apart by the size of him.

But I was going to come again, and I couldn't come with anything inside me. I knew that. It was an indelible fact.

"I'm coming inside you," he gasped. "I'm going to come so fucking hard in you."

"Me too." I didn't even believe it. "You're making me come."

The swirl of feeling dropped away then coalesced, increasing until my limbs stiffened and I put my face in his neck to stifle my cries. The impossible happened. I came just from a man inside me. I pulsed around him, drowning in the power of it.

He thrust hard with a grunt then a moan. I felt the pulse at the base of his dick on my stretched pussy. He was coming. Making that beautiful man lose himself in me felt like a gift. I pushed into him until he slowed, stopped, and kissed my neck.

"*Grazie*," he said.

"You're welcome."

Slowly, he slipped his dick out of me. It was still rigid, and I felt every inch of it against my raw skin. He tied off the condom and wrapped it in toilet paper as I sat up.

"Stay there," he said, pressing my legs open.

Was he going to have me again? I didn't think I could take it. Though I was already feeling twinges of shame and guilt, I wouldn't have turned him down. He balled up a wad of tissue and pressed it between my legs, cleaning me. The gesture was so much more intimate than the actual sex that I blushed.

"I can't send you back outside with sex dripping down your leg, now can I?"

Despite the sounds from the party, I'd forgotten that there would be a "back outside." I'd forgotten about Daniel, his meek request that I come back to him, and the air of forgiveness my attendance was supposed to provide. I closed my legs and sat up.

"I have to get back out there." I put my left shoe on all the way and popped off the vanity. "Thank you."

"My pleasure."

The shreds of my underwear tickled my inner thighs, bunching as only ripped lace could. I straightened my skirt and smoothed my stockings, knowing he was watching me. I didn't look at him as I went for the door.

He slipped between me and the knob. "Contessa."

"Yes?"

"Don't leave like this."

"How should I leave?"

He kissed my forehead, and I let myself enjoy the tenderness. I didn't want to rush out, but I couldn't delude myself into thinking I was fully present, either.

"It doesn't have to be meaningless," he said.

"You won't answer questions about your life, and I'm still in love with my ex. I don't know how it can be meaningful."

"I'll answer one question right now if you kiss me back like you mean it."

"Why are you doing this? You're the one who wanted two bodies meeting and no more."

"Because I can't walk out of this room like this. You're like a stranger all of a sudden. One question."

"The girl. Who was she? To you, I mean? Why did you come here for her?"

"That's three questions."

"Pick one."

"My sister. She's my sister. Her name is Nella."

"And?"

He bit his lip and looked down at my face. After a second, I realized he wasn't going to answer me.

"Excuse me." I pushed him away, but he shoved me against the door.

"I want my kiss," he said.

"That was no kind of answer."

"I answered two of the three. If you only cared about the last one, you should have said so."

"Lawyer." I said it like an indictment, and he smirked. I elbowed him, but he caught my forearms and pinned me to the door.

"Your underwear's already ripped, and if I checked, I bet you're wet again."

"Get off me," I said.

"I should fuck you right now."

"Go to hell."

I twisted, but his hands were bruising, and the growing hardness of his dick was enough to weaken my knees and my resolve. "Take your kiss then."

He did, without hesitation or gentleness, prying my mouth open with his tongue, thick with the taste of my pussy. He pulled away when we had to breathe, and we stared at each other, panting.

"I hope you enjoyed that," I said. "Now excuse me."

He backed away from the door, and I went through it before he and his beautiful dick could stop me. The air outside the bathroom felt fresher and thinner. I smoothed my dress again and pulled the pins out of my hair, letting it fall down in a red cascade. It was easier to keep that way.

I felt a weight between my legs. I could easily get my appearance together for the rest of the party. But I couldn't hide the fact that my cheeks were pink with arousal and my nipples stood on end. My arms still had goose bumps, and I was so wet I felt the moisture inside my thighs. But I walked outside as if it were my house, my party, my world, because that's what I did. It was easier than math.

Dinner had started. Daniel was at his table with an empty seat next to him. He hadn't mentioned the seating arrangements, but they shouldn't have surprised me. Forgiveness didn't sit across the room. He stood as I took my seat.

"Thank you," I said. When our eyes met, I was sure he knew what I'd just done.

Chapter 12.

The next morning, two things happened simultaneously. One. A dozen red roses on Pam's desk.

"Wow, these from Bobby?" I asked.

"They're for you." She tapped a pen to the desk blotter, as if writing a song in her head.

Before I could open the paper flap of the card, the second thing happened. I caught the image on my assistant's screen of Antonio and me in the hallway. It had been shot through the window the moment before we kissed. Next to that image was one of Daniel and me sitting together at dinner.

I'd feared looking weak. I'd feared the op ed pieces about my neediness and desperation, about Daniel's ambition and mindless drive for power. The inevitable comparisons to greater women's choices about cheating political mates. Maybe I should have worried about looking like a whore.

"Who's that?" Pam asked.

Who was he? I ran the question over and over in my mind, and I didn't have an acceptable answer. He was a man I'd met the other day. He was a magnet for my sexual hunger.

"He's being investigated for fraud," Pam said, as if he was just a guy on the screen and not someone I had been standing so close to I could feel his heat. "Is he the same guy with the cars?"

"Same," I choked. "What's the article say?" I opened the envelope so I wouldn't have to look at the screen. I figured the flowers were from Daniel, asking for another reprieve.

"Says you and Antonio Spinelli are friends through WDE. And you're reconciling with Daniel Brower."

"They used that word? Reconciling?" I looked at the card.

One more question.

No name. An arrogant avoidance of redundancy. I folded it back into the envelope.

"Yeppers," Pam said. "Right next to that picture with the hot Italian guy. Sneaky."

"Journalist. In Latin it means 'to say everything while saying nothing.'"

"Really?"

"No. But if the ancients had known anything at all, it would."

***

I'd gotten up and dressed like any other morning, expecting nothing more than the usual inconveniences. Traffic. Runny stockings. Coffee too hot/cold. Daniel and I had parted amicably the previous night, with him whispering "think about it," in my ear. I promised to, and I would, but it was hard to think of Daniel when I woke up with a soaked, sore pussy courtesy of Antonio.

I relieved myself, fingers stroking the soreness. I loved the pain of remembrance. He'd been so good, so hard, and talking during sex was something new. I whispered to myself *fuck me fuck me fuck me hard* until I came, ass tightening, hips twisting, balancing my whole body on the top of my head and the balls of my feet.

Only when I took my first panting breaths, cupping myself in my palm, did I consider how poorly we'd parted. I couldn't be with someone so closed off. Later at work, when Pam told me he was under investigation, I knew why he didn't like being interrogated. I had her hold my calls for an hour.

One more question.

What would it be? More about Nella? Another reason to land in Los Angeles besides easy Bar exams? No. All that was too facile and obviously loaded for him. I locked my office door. I had a million things to do, but none would happen while those pictures sat in my mind. I needed to solve all of it immediately with an internet search.

If I could have bottled the next hour in a fragrance, it would have been called frustration. If the size of the bottle contained the amount of information I found on Antonio Spinelli, it would be one ounce, not a drop more, and the contents would be worth less than the vessel.

In other words, one sidebar article in *Fortune* had not one undigested word. I found one professional photograph in which he looked gorgeous, an unsubstantiated complaint in the comment section of a real estate blog bitching about how many cars he had and how much property he owned, a short fluff piece about Zia Giovana in the *San Pedro Sun,* and an investigative piece in the same paper from two years later.

The investigative piece was recent enough to matter. Antonio Spinelli, owner and proprietor of Zia's restaurant, was under investigation for laundering millions through the establishment. The claim was absolutely impossible to prove, and apparently the money trail died before the reporter's deadline.

Pam texted me.

—*Mister Brower is on the line*—

—*I have another twenty minutes*—

—*He's pretty insistent*—

Pam knew me, and she knew my ex-fiancé. She wouldn't interrupt for nonsense. I picked up the phone.

"Hi," I said.

He started before I had the chance to take another breath.

"What are you doing?"

"What?"

"With a known criminal. What are you doing with him?"
I was shocked into speechlessness.
"Tink? Answer me. It was in the *LA Times*."
"I'm not *with* anyone. Not that it's your business."
"Your safety is my business. I'm sorry. That's not negotiable now or ever."

His voice seemed physically present, coming through not just the phone but the walls, and I realized he was right outside my locked door.

"Let me in," he said.

I hung up and opened the door. "You have to relax." It was barely out of my mouth before he slammed the door and shut out his bodyguards, who seemed to be holding back Pam.

"Daniel, really—"

"Really? Really, Theresa? Where did you pick him up?"

I put my hands on my hips. I had to bite my lips to keep in all the pointless recrimination. We didn't need more of it. Daniel knew things.

"Do you want to take it easy and talk to me?" I said.

"No," he said, taking my shoulders. "I don't." He kissed me, pushing me back against my desk.

I kept my mouth closed not out of anger, but confusion. By the time he pulled back, we'd both calmed down.

"I'm sorry," he said.

"Sit down." I indicated the chair across from my desk, and I sat next to it.

He pulled his chair close to mine as if he was still entitled to breathe my air, as if I'd agreed to the newspaper's reconciliation in real life. "I need you to tell me everything," he said, gathering my hands.

"There's nothing to tell."

"How did he approach you?"

I pulled my hands away. "This is not fair. You're not exactly entitled to any information about me or my love life anymore. If I tell you it's nothing, you're going to think I'm lying. If I tell you it's something, it's like I'm trying to hurt you. I'm just trying to live my life, okay? I'm just trying to get through my days and nights."

"You're stumbling into a place where you can get hurt."

"All roads lead to hurt, trust me."

"I deserved that."

"It wasn't directed at you." I threw his hands off me. "Can I just talk to you without all the baggage?"

"No, because you've forgotten who you are."

"I'm not yours anymore."

"You're an heiress. A socialite. You run one of the biggest accounting departments in Hollywood. You funnel millions of dollars a day. You have access to the district attorney."

"This is about *you?*"

"No! Fuck!" The curse was pure exclamation. Not a lead in or a modifier.

He paused for half of a microsecond, but I caught it. When he and I were together, I hadn't liked cursing. I thought he didn't do it until I found his texts to Clarice, and I found out just how well he used the word fuck.

He put his elbows on his knees and put his face in his hands. "He's the capo of the Giraldi crime family, Tinkerbell."

If I'd had a muscle in my body that wasn't tensed to pain, they caught up. Even my toes curled. "You're making that up."

His face was red and sweaty. He looked more like a man and less like a mayor than he had since the morning I discovered his infidelity. "I wish I was. I wish I was only jealous."

My ex-fiancé didn't get jealous often, but when he did, he burned white hot. I'd never betrayed him or any of my boyfriends. My relationships had ended because of educational choices (Randolph went to Berkeley, and I went to MIT) or because the other party strayed or because there was nothing worth bothering with, as was the case with Sam Traulich. He was a nice guy, just completely incompatible with me.

Sam and I stayed friends, and when he'd called to ask if I had any contacts at Northwestern Films, I agreed to a lunch. It had gone long. At three thirty p.m., Sam and I were laughing over some crumb of nostalgia when Daniel stormed into the little diner. At first, he was thrilled to see me alive. He'd apparently been calling the office for hours about our dinner plans, and no one knew where I was. My cell battery had died, so he tracked me down by having his friends on First Street look into my credit card transactions for the previous two hours.

For some reason, that didn't bother me.

Once he'd gotten over his initial delight, he got a good look at Sam, who was burnished brown from the sun, joyful as always, laid-back, and in good humor. Daniel put on his politician game, apologized, and appeared to forget about it. We made it to dinner on time. Life moved on.

But not for Daniel. I was shocked to find out years later, through a mutual friend, what had followed. As an extraordinarily popular young prosecutor, Daniel had arranged for Sam to be picked up by the police, brought in, roughed up, and detained. Daniel visited the detainee and mentioned that if he ever kept his girlfriend too long again, Sam would be joined in his cell by at least three gang members who owed him favors.

I had been livid. I slept on the couch for three weeks and barely spoke to him. That was the last intolerably stupid thing Daniel ever did on my behalf.

"Okay," I said. "I'm listening. Antonio is what... in the mafia?"

"Yes."

"You mean there's still a mafia?"

"Yes, Virginia, there is a mafia."

I paused for a long time. On the one hand, he might as well have told me Antonio was a leprechaun. On the other, I couldn't say I was surprised.

Chapter 13.

I texted Antonio.

—I have my one question—

—I want you to ask it in person—

—Agreed—

The address was in Hollywood Heights, overlooking the Bowl, on a hairpin turn that looked like a sheer drop on the right and a fortress wall on the left. A thirty-foot long, fifteen-foot high dumpster was visible over the hedge, and crashing and banging drowned out the scrape of cricket wings. I edged past a pickup truck that looked as though it had survived a demolition derby and parked next to a low sports car covered by a grey tarp.

The house was Spanish with a red tile roof, leaded stained glass accents, and thick adobe walls. Tarps swung from rafters, and every wall's plaster had been cracked down to the lathe. I followed the banging and crashing, nodding at the rough men pushing a wheelbarrow of broken house detritus.

"Is Antonio here?" I asked.

I couldn't imagine him hanging around a scraped-to-the-beams structure, but one of the guys thumbed toward the back of the house. I thanked him and headed in that direction. The pounding, thumping sounds were followed by the tickle of pebbles hitting the floor. The air got dusty, and the smell of pine hit me as I saw him.

I'd always been attracted to clean cut, educated men, men who had people to change their flat tires, drive them around, break down their walls. They exerted themselves mightily in gyms and squash courts. But none of them had ever looked like Antonio. He hoisted a sledgehammer and brought it down. The wall crumbled under the weight, and he wedged the head behind the wall and yanked it out, sending a shot of plaster and shredded lathe toward him. He didn't stop, though. Didn't even pause. His wiry muscles shifted and pulsed. The satin sheen of sweat on his olive skin brought out every muscle and tendon.

I knew women who liked that sort of thing: a sweaty man doing physical labor. I had never understood the appeal until that moment. He brought the sledgehammer down with a coil of force, like a righteous god smiting an errant creation off the face of his earth. The movement was so dramatic the gold pendant around his neck swung around to his shoulder.

"I know you're there, Contessa." He brought the hammer down again.

"Don't you have people to do this for you?"

He tossed the hammer down as if he was done with the day's violence. "It's my house, and demo's too much fun to delegate." His face was covered in dust, sweat, and a smile.

"You should hire yourself," I said.

"Like it?"

"It'll be nice once you mop. Dust. You know, maybe a few pictures on the wall." I swept my hand to the view of the city, the busted everything, the sheer potential.

"Let me show you." He headed out an archway, indicating I should follow.

He led me onto a balcony on the west side of the house. The terra-cotta floor looked to be in good shape, and the cast-iron railing curled in on itself, making a floral design I'd never seen.

"I love this view," I said, understating the grandeur of the ocean of lights. "I could look out on this all night."

He pulled a pack of cigarettes from his back pocket and poked one out. I refused his offer, and he took out a big metal lighter.

"Sit here at night, have a glass of wine. Or in the morning, a cup of coffee, just look over the city." He lit his cigarette with a *click* clack, his profile something out of an art history class. He put his fingertips to the back of my neck, his stroke so delicate I didn't lean into it, just stayed as still as I could.

"You had a question?" he asked, tracing the line where my shirt met my skin.

"Are you a leprechaun?" I asked.

"Only when St. Patrick's Day lands on a full moon." He was smiling, but I could see the question had confused him.

"I'm sorry. I had a real question, but I forgot which one I picked."

Because they were all ridiculous, of course. If he was some cartoon capo, he'd have a dozen guys around him all the time. He'd wear pinstripes and a fedora. He'd carry a gun. He'd say *capisce* a lot.

"Do I get any questions?" he asked, interrupting my thoughts.

"I'm an open book."

He laughed softly, smoke trailing behind him. "Right. Open, but in a different language."

He gave me an idea.

"I'm not going to ask you a question," I said. "I'm going to tell you what happened to me today."

"Let me make you coffee."

***

The kitchen was in bad but useable shape. The beige marbled tiles with little mirrored squares every few feet, dark wood cabinets, and avocado appliances told me the place hadn't been redone since the seventies.

Antonio sat me in a folding chair at a beat up pine table. "Best I have for now."

"You living here during all this mess?"

"No. I have another place." He gave no more information. "Do you like espresso? I have some hot still."

"Sure."

He poured from a chrome double brewer into two small blue cups. "Does it keep you up?"

"Nope."

"Good. A real woman." He brought the cups and a lemon to the table and set a cup before me. I reached for the handle, but he made a little *tch tch* noise. "Not yet." He cradled the lemon in one palm and a little knife in the other. "What happened to you today?"

"Today, my assistant found a picture of us in the paper."

"Saw that," he said, cutting a strip of lemon peel. "You looked sexy as hell. I wanted to fuck you all over again."

If he was trying to get my body to turn into a puddle of desire, it was working. "Everyone saw it."

"Everyone want to fuck you as bad as I did?"

"My ex-fiancé showed up."

"The Candidate..." He dropped a yellow curlicue into my saucer. "Bet he regrets what he did, no?"

"You'll have to ask him."

I reached for the espresso, but he stopped me again, plucking the rind from my saucer and rubbing it on the edge of my cup.

"Do you want Sambuca?" he asked.

"Sure."

He reached back, plucked a bottle from a line of them, and unscrewed the top. "In Napoli, the men point their pinkies up when they drink espresso to show their refinement. Once they've been here long enough, they drink like Americans." He poured a little Sambuca into our cups.

"How do the women drink?"

"Quickly, before the children pull on their skirts."

I sipped the drink. It was good, thick, rich. I took a bigger mouthful but didn't gulp.

"So there's a picture in the paper of us, and let's not play tricks with each other," he said. "It looked like we're intimate."

"It did."

"Next to a picture of you and him." He picked up his cup. I followed suit. "Yes."

"And he runs to your office, how many hours later? One? A half? Or are we measuring in minutes?"

We looked at each other over our cups.

"I don't see that it matters." I blew on the black liquid, the ripples releasing the licorice scent of the Sambuca.

He smirked. "Maybe it doesn't. What did it take him one to sixty minutes to tell you?"

"That you run an organized crime empire."

He said nothing at first, just put his espresso to his lips and drank. He kept his pinky down, holding the demitasse with his curled fist. "I'm very impressed with me." He clicked the cup to saucer. "Less so with him. I might have to vote Drummond."

"I looked into it after he left, once I knew what I was looking for. You're being investigated for all kinds of fraud. Insurance. Real estate. And you don't want me to ask questions, so what am I supposed to think?"

"Is that your question?" he asked. "What are you supposed to think? I have an answer for that one."

"I don't have an actual question. I know you haven't been convicted of anything, and I know what we had was just a casual screw."

"It wasn't casual."

"We can't make any commitments to each other. And that's fine. But I don't sleep with strangers. If you're going to continue to be a stranger, then I can't do this."

He closed his eyes and cocked his head left, then right, as if stretching before a boxing match. "I have a history, and it followed me here."

I sat back. "Go on."

"My father didn't exist to me. My mother shooed off the idea of him. Like she made me herself, out of nothing. I didn't know who my father was until I was eleven. I had some business, and he was the man one went to with business."

"At eleven? What business did you have at that age?"

"It's a different world over there. Things need to be taken care of. If the trash wasn't getting picked up, you went to Benito Racossi. If the delivery boy was stealing from your mother, you went to Racossi. My mother rarely left the apartment, and my sister... Well, I'd never send her to a man like that. But once I met him, I saw it." He made a quick oval around his face. "Like looking in a mirror, but older."

"He was your father?"

"He didn't deny it. Took me under his wing. Gave me work. Legal work. Anything he had to keep me out of trouble. My mother? It nearly killed her. She didn't want me in the life. She never believed I didn't do anything illegal. Neither did the *polizia*. Neither did Interpol. Neither does Daniel Brower, who's going to make my life hell if he's mayor. But as God is my witness, every business I have runs because I watched how my father did it, but I've never imitated what he did. So I'll tell you this once and swear to it, I've beaten every charge against me and I'll beat everything they put on my back because I'm clean."

"I believe you."

"Don't put me in a position where I have to defend myself against this again."

He was so definite, so stern, so parental that I didn't think I could spend another second in his presence. I stood. "If asking you questions turns you into an ass, I'll be sure to only make declarative statements on the infinitely small chance I ever see you again. Thanks for the coffee."

I spun on my heel and walked out of the kitchen, winding up in a room I hadn't come through. Then I found another with a broken stone staircase. I didn't feel him following me until a second before he grabbed me and pushed me toward a leaded glass window.

"Let go of me."

"No."

I clawed at his hands as they fondled me, going under my shirt and bra without prelude or hesitation. The flood of arousal was painful.

"Stop," I said, trying to get his arms off me.

"Next time you say stop will be the last." He placed my hands on either side of the window. The stone was cold, and the pressure of him on my back was harder than the wall. "What do you want to say?" He shifted behind me, unmistakably getting his dick out. I heard the tick of a condom wrapper hitting the tiles. Was he wrapping it up again? God, I hoped so.

I wanted to say stop. No. Don't. But I needed him to relieve my ache, and I knew he meant that my next objection would send him away. "Do it."

He yanked down my pants. I saw his reflection in the window, broken by curved strips of lead, looking at my ass. He put one hand on my throat, his thumb resting behind my ear, while his other hand yanked down my underwear and drove into where I was wettest.

"I'm going to fuck you so fucking hard." He tightened the grip of both hands.

I'd made him angry. That was clear in every vowel. I shouldn't like that. It shouldn't turn me on. But as I stood with my ass jutting out, my bra and shirt pulled up until my breasts swung, and a man's dick at my opening, I could only wonder how to make him angrier.

"You'd better make it worthwhile," I said. "I have no time for sweet talk."

"You're such a rich little princess." He pressed my neck down and pulled my hips toward him with the fingers he had inserted in me.

"Fuck you," I whispered. "You're a worthless street punk."

I thought he would put his dick back in his pants and walk away. Instead, he jammed it in me with animal brutality. I cried out not because it hurt, but because the way he did it, plus the raw physical pleasure it created, pushed the wind out of me.

"You like this?" he said, thrusting with every word. "You like this. Worthless. Street. Punk. Fucking. You?"

His arms constricted around me. His right squeezed a breast, his left had four fingers on my clit, shifting like tectonic plates with every thrust. I grunted. I didn't think I'd ever grunted during sex, but that wasn't sex. That was two animals mating under a bush.

He pulled out and yanked me up. I saw us in the reflection in the window.

"Look at you. That face. I want to see you when you come." He growled it. "Since the minute I saw you, I've wanted you. I've wanted to open your legs and take you." As if his words were fingers, they drifted down my body, fondling me, arousing me. "I've seen women come. They forget to look beautiful. They forget who they are. I want to see you when you lose yourself and all you know is my name."

He sat on the windowsill, holding his hand out for me. I straddled him, lowering myself onto him. He guided me by the hips.

"This is good?" he asked as if he already knew the answer.

"So good. Fucking you is so good."

"Look at me."

He pressed me down, pressing my clit against his root. I gasped, trying to keep my eyes on him.

"Let me see," he whispered over and over. "Let me see you come."

He fucked harder and faster, and I lost myself.

"Oh God," I gasped. "Coming. Coming."

"Give it to me, Contessa. Show me."

He put his hand under my chin, pushing it up until my vision was filled with him. I opened my mouth, but nothing came out. My lungs constricted around my heart, and my joints stiffened. I felt held up by his dick, but his arms and hands bound me to him as I came, watching him.

I pressed my forehead to his shoulder and put my hands on his biceps, and without an ounce of tenderness, he pulled my hair back and down until I was on my knees with the slick head of his cock against my cheek, and he stood over me.

"Take it. Now."

He pulled the condom off. I opened my mouth, and he guided himself in. I choked, and he pulled out. I prepared myself, holding down my reflex and pressing the back of my tongue down.

I put my hands at the base of his shaft and put his cock in my mouth, sliding the bottom of it against my flattened tongue. As he slid it out, I sucked, tasting my fluids on him.

"Yes, Contessa, that's it. Suck my cock. All the way."

I took him into my throat as far as I could, making up the rest with my hands, and sucked as he pulled out.

"Look at me," he said.

We made eye contact, and he pushed forward. I opened my throat, but he was a lot of man for one mouth. I paused and, again, took him far down. His lips parted, and I knew I'd done it right. He thrust into me. He felt good, tasted good. I wanted him to come hard, and my desire to please him rattled the back of my throat.

"I'm coming in your mouth." He grunted. "Take it. Take it all in your throat."

His eyes closed tight, and I watched him as he thrust and came, flooding my tongue and throat with bitter, sticky lava. He muttered something in Italian, spitting curses through his teeth. I'd never seen anything so hot, and I swallowed every drop of him.

When he opened his eyes and saw me beneath him, he took a sharp breath. "So sweet." He brushed my hair away from my face then pulled my head to him.

I didn't even understand my reactions. "Not casual. I know what you mean."

"But no questions. It means I have to defend myself. I don't like it."

"Okay. No more questions." I didn't know if I could keep that promise, but I could definitely put it on hold to have sex like that again.

I turned, wrapping my arms around his legs, and I turned to watch the image of us, me on my knees before him, with his hands at my back, in the window.

I screamed. Like a glowing mask floating in the night, a woman's face sat framed in the window.

Chapter 14.

Antonio had me behind him so quickly and smoothly I didn't even realize he was protecting me until I tried to stand. My pants restricted my thighs, and I nearly fell.

He held me up. "Marina!" he shouted.

I straightened my shirt and pants. Antonio zipped himself up and ran for the door.

He turned and held up a finger to me. "Don't go anywhere."

And he was gone. I still had the sting of his spunk in the back of my throat.

I straightened, breathed, and went outside. His admonition to stay put had fallen on Teflon ears. I didn't know who Marina was or what she was doing outside his window. She could be a sister or cousin or the local convent rep, but she was young and attractive, and my blood went a familiar shade of green. I didn't like feeling that way, especially about a man I had no claim to.

I intended to get in my car and drive away. Around the bend, I found the balcony. I knew how to get back to my car from there, but I heard voices. A Mercedes was parked in the rear drive, lights on and engine running. The woman stood by the open driver's door. She was upset, hands flailing, voice squeaking. Antonio shouted recriminations in the spaces between hers.

That wasn't a fight between cousins. I stepped back, and my foot shifted a loose tile. The scrape was louder than I would have imagined. They looked up at me. I backed away then turned and ran to my car. I managed to get in my car and get it started before he got to the window. He knocked on the glass. I waved good-bye.

He got in front of the car. "Open up."

I cranked down the window. "That only works during, not after."

"It's not what you think."

"Is she a blood relation?"

He came around to my side of the car.

"Yes? No? What is it, Antonio? Oh, I'm sorry. Did I phrase that as a question?"

I put the car in gear, and he threw himself through my open window. I screamed from the shock of having him between me and the windshield. He yanked the emergency brake.

"Don't make me drag you out of this car," he said.

"If you have something to tell me, just tell me. I'm not asking anything."

"Come inside."

"No."

Still leaning through the door, he held the bottom of my face. "I want you. First, I want you."

"Thanks. I'm glad I'm not a second. You know what? I'm tired of playing in an orchestra. I want to go solo. Now." I pulled the brake down. "Get out of my car, or half of you is getting torn off when I drive away."

"It's not what you think."

I put the car in drive. "You have no idea what I think."

I let go of the brake, and even though I couldn't see through Antonio's gorgeous body, I drove. He cursed and pulled out of the window. I turned onto the street and left him behind.

Chapter 15.

"What's your problem?" Katrina asked three days later.

We were on set in Elysian Park from seven a.m. to three p.m. on a weekend, and the light had been consistently softened by clouds. I shrugged. I had no idea what she was talking about. I still had to go through the other script supervisor's notes.

She put her knee on the park bench where I had set up my files. "You got a frown." She formed her hand into a claw and pivoted her wrist as if turning a knob on my face. "It needs an inversion."

Pam had called it a sourpuss, and I'd given her the same answer. "I'm fine. Just a cold."

"Bullshit." She was fatigued. The days were very long, and she had confided that she was losing faith that it would ever be a movie. It was a common malady at the seventy-five percent mark. "I don't have time to needle it out of you because in two minutes, someone is going to come here asking me which shirt Michael should wear, and I'll have to convince them I care. So tell me."

I slapped the clipboard on the table. "The Italian guy. He gave every indication he didn't want me close. I slept with him twice, neither time in an actual bed, and I'm an idiot for being shocked that I wasn't the only one he was with. So no, I expected nothing from him. But maybe once, for kicks, I'd like someone to be exclusive for fifteen minutes."

"Ah."

"Fuck it. I don't care."

She stood still for a second then said, "Did you just say what I think you said?"

I flipped through my pages without looking at her. "Go direct a movie. You make me crazy."

She stepped away from the table, walking backward to the camera. When she was far enough away, I checked my phone. That text was the first I'd heard from Antonio since I almost tore him in half with my car.

—I'd like to speak with you—

—I'm all out of questions—

—I'll do the talking—

What was he promising? More non-answers? That game was old. Either he would be forthcoming or he wouldn't, and the more he promised to reveal who he really was, the less appealing he became. I needed overall sincerity. I needed intimacy. I didn't need a sex doll, no matter how good the sex was.

—No. I'm sorry. I'm done with this—

—But I'm not—

I shuddered and pocketed the phone. I wasn't going to encourage him.

Michael threw himself into the chair next to me, his lithe, tight body encased in a henley and grey jeans. "Heard that conversation back there."

"And you have the answer?"

"I have *an* answer. Wanna hear it?" He raised his eyebrows as if he was offering candy. He was a handsome guy, and twice as fine on camera.

"Sure."

"It's not you, it's him."

I laughed.

Michael leaned forward. "I mean it. Look, I'm... let's say active. It's not the girls. Some are real nice. Good people. Make someone a great wife. But I'm on set until the wee hours. I can't do the maintenance a guy's gotta do. So we're clear on that in the beginning."

"You're a charmer, you know that?"

"Any time. And if you want to be clear about something, some time, we can be maintenance-free. You and I."

"I'm this close to taking my pants off and jumping on you. I mean, you can really sell a girl."

He laughed, shaking his head. "All right. But friend to friend, it's not you. You're very cool, very beautiful, very smart. Just unlucky so far." He bounced up and gave me a salute. "Remember all that. And if you're ever looking, let me know."

"Thanks. I mean it."

He strode off to makeup. I checked my phone. Antonio didn't send a follow-up, and I didn't answer. Michael had cheered me up somewhat. He was all right, and maybe if I wanted something forgettable sometime, I'd call him.

The park shoot bled into Sunday, and I collapsed on my couch with a duffel bag full of binders and notebooks at my feet. Katrina dropped her head on the kitchen table with the TV on.

Chapter 16.

Our Monday meeting had been a drone of problems and the same processes to manage them. Then we talked about implementing new processes to manage the same issues. Then we had new discussion points that were just shades of the old ones. The agency collected money on behalf of clients, deducted ten percent, and sent the rest. Anytime money moved, there were the twin matters of how much and how fast it moved. Nothing else really counted.

When I came back, Pam tapped her fingers like a drum machine, hitting the stapler on fourths. "Danny Dickinsonian."

"Is he here?" I asked.

"Nope. Wanted you to meet him at his office downtown. Said it was important and apologies for the imposition et cetera. New polls show he's getting beaten on the east side. Badly. Might be about that." Tap tap tappa.

Running for mayor was an eighty-hour-a-week job. I'd known that from the beginning. "What do I have this afternoon?"

"Staff meeting at one. Procedure and protocols touchbase with Wanda's team at two."

Taking an afternoon jaunt downtown was undoubtedly ten times more appealing than either of those events. "Tell him I'll be there."

***

The DA's office was in a 1920s stone-carved edifice a few blocks from my loft, so I parked at home and walked. The heat weighed on me. The streets, though not crowded, were populated.

The DA's building was set back from the street with an expanse of lawn utilized by birds, squirrels, and urban picnickers. The tweedy grey brickwork matched the flat city sky, and as I got closer, I saw the stonework from a lost era. Like Roman reliefs, granite men carried logs, fished in a pebble sea, built houses from petrified wood, all immortalized with the toil of a sculptor's sweat.

The lady at the front desk knew me, but I still needed to sign in and get a sticker. I was spared the thumbprint. I saw Gerry, Daniel's top strategist, in the hall.

He stopped short and put out his hand. "Theresa, thank you for going to Catholic Charities." When he shook my hand, he also kissed my cheek and patted my back.

"I was afraid I did more harm than good," I said.

"No. Even a failed tactic can serve an overall strategy. Don't forget that."

"So I'm a failed tactic now?" I said with a smile and a lilt. "I thought I meant more to you than that."

He pressed his lips together. "You're perfect. You have politics in your blood. If I could, in good conscience, ask you to take that stupid bastard back, I would. He can't lose with you by him."

I had a few answers, none of them politic or kind. I chose the most bland. "He can win just fine without me."

"Maybe, but it'll be close."

"Any idea why I'm here?"

"Come," he said.

I let him lead me down the hall to Daniel's office. A married couple he used for promotion was just leaving. They greeted me, then suddenly I was alone with my ex-fiancé.

He had a biggish office by 1920s standards. The windows slid up and down with rackety tick*tick*s, and the walls were molded in every place molding could be placed. Over the last ninety years, it had been painted bi-annually, rounding out the edges until the room looked like the inside of a wedding cake.

"Found her wandering the halls," Gerry said before ducking out.

Daniel had on a thin blue tie and white shirt with the cuffs rolled to the elbows. His wooden chair was dressed in his jacket, and he was every bit the good-looking, hardworking crusader for justice. "Theresa, thank you for coming."

"After the election, this beck-and-call thing is over," I said.

He approached a chestnut table that must have come with the building and pulled out a chair for me. I sat. He leaned on his desk and crossed his arms instead of sitting with me. I crossed my legs and faced him.

"It's been a tough few days here," he said.

"I have a protocol review I can still make if you don't have something to say to me."

"I know how much you love those." He smiled his big, natural white smile.

"There were threats something would actually get done at this one."

"Then it's not really a protocol review."

I sighed. "This is about Antonio again? Just say it."

"I need to know what he is to you."

"Oh, God. Really?" I stood. "Dan, honey, you're so far out of line."

"It matters. It matters to my campaign, and it matters to me. I need your help, and in order for me to even ask, I need to know the nature of your relationship with him."

"It's nothing."

"Have you had sex with him?"

"Daniel!"

"I need to know."

"Is this a deposition? Are you taking notes? Where's the court reporter?"

He sighed and dropped his arms. "We've reached a wonderful pause in a war that's been going on for a few decades. We have the Carlonis for all manner of shit, and I'll file charges when everything's in order. But the other side? The Giraldi family? I have nothing. I have accounting files we got from the NSA, but everything looks clean. I need them looked at by someone with your eye."

"And you don't have a team of people?"

"They have skill. You have talent."

"I think this is about more than my talent." I couldn't hold to that line for long because he'd asked me to look at the Carloni files months ago. He'd switched to their rivals, but his ideals about my talents were well known.

"We got Donna Maria Carloni on embezzlement thanks to a mole. Good mole. I got nothing with Spinelli," he said.

"Who you can't even prove is the head of any kind of crime organization, much less the Giraldis."

"He's committed a few murders to get to where he is, Tink. Just because I can't prove it doesn't make it any less true. And yes, I'm terrified of you being anywhere near him, and yes, this is two birds with one stone. I get your eyes on his books, and I get *you* to tell *me* where his malfeasance is. But if you're sleeping with him, I can't use you. I'll have to fly a guy in from Quantico, and that'll alert everyone that I have the NSA docs. They'll be questioned and possibly yanked."

"This is a hot mess."

"I know."

"The only way for me to avoid drama is to walk out right now," I said. "But you have me curious. And you know I think you're the best man for the mayor's mansion."

"So will you?"

"I had sex with him twice. But it's over."

He looked down to hide his expression, but I saw his fingers tighten. My first reaction was to tell him tough crap. He threw me away. It was my right to sleep with anyone I wanted. My second reaction was subtler.

"Do you have time for a personal question?" I asked.

He looked at me. I'd hurt him. I loved him, and I'd hurt him. I knew how he felt when he did it to me.

"I need it answered completely and honestly," I said. "I have no energy for beating around the bush or confidence boosts right now."

"Okay."

"Is something about me just not enough? I mean, is there something inherently unsatisfying?"

He took a long time answering. "I always wondered if you really enjoyed it."

I picked up my bag and slung it over my shoulder. "I did. A lot."

He rushed to open the door for me. "I'm avoiding asking for another chance."

"Well done, Mister Mayor."

***

I got back to WDE in time for the protocol review, which was marginally productive. When I got back to my office, another vase of red roses stood on Pam's desk.

I don't give up so easy

Yeah. He'd chase me, catch me, and continue with Marina or whoever else made him feel good. An inaccessible little heiress would quickly become boring.

After seven years, Daniel didn't know if I'd enjoyed sex. What was wrong with me? Was I empty inside? I'd thought I'd imagined every horrifying answer he could have given me, but I hadn't even scratched the surface.

At least I knew what the problem was. Maybe if I went back to Daniel with the assurance that I did like sex, he wouldn't look elsewhere. Maybe. But the thought of going back to him just depressed me.

Chapter 17.

I woke to the smell of bacon. I'd somehow crawled into bed during the middle of the night. Katrina had been known to put breakfast together when she felt chipper, and I was very grateful for her mood and her hospitality, especially on a work day. I showered and put up my hair, masking the circles under my eyes with some very expensive stage makeup. I was mid-stairwell when I heard a man's voice coming from the open kitchen. Katrina said something I couldn't hear above the crackle of pork belly. Then the man laughed.

"Antonio?" I bent around the iron bannister.

"He said I have to call him Spin," Katrina called.

"*Buongiorno*! I brought you breakfast."

I stepped into the kitchen. "I smelled the bacon."

"It's pancetta," Katrina said, picking a few squares out of the pan and putting them on toast. "He's corrected me, like, seven times already. He's cute but annoying."

"Mostly annoying," he said, shifting scrambled eggs across the pan.

"Annoy me any time." She folded up her sandwich and slipped it into a bag.

"This is a little presumptuous considering the way we left it last time," I said.

"Gotta go!" Katrina gave Antonio the one-kiss-per-cheek exit and bounced out with a wink to me.

I crossed my arms, but I was hungry. The pancetta smelled delicious.

Antonio pointed the fork at me. "This suit? It's nice for a funeral."

I sucked in my cheeks. I'd chosen a black below-the-knee wool skirt and matching jacket, and he was trying to throw me off in my own house. He looked perfect in a light blue sweater and collar shirt.

"Insulting me?" I stood next to him and bumped him with my hip. "This is how you seduce me?" I snapped a wooden spoon from the canister and poked at the eggs.

"If I wanted to seduce you, the suit would be on the floor already."

"You don't want to seduce me?"

He took a piece of egg on a fork and blew on it. "I do, but as you know, we left on poor terms last time." He held the fork to my lips, holding his palm under it to catch if it dripped.

"And tell me, Mister Spinelli, how do you intend to improve the terms?" I let him feed me.

"By explaining." He divided the eggs onto two plates.

"What? I can't hear you over this explosion of delicious."

He looked genuinely pleased that I liked his cooking, and he counted the ingredients on his fingers. "Salt, milk, *parmesano*, rosemary, and pancetta, of course. You have all my secrets now." He put the plates on the center island and pulled a stool out for me. He'd already set out coffee, juice, and toast.

"You've buttered me up quite thoroughly."

He sat and poured me coffee. "A compliment for a job well done?"

"Yes."

"I appreciate that. But I want to give you the explanation part now, if the taste of the eggs won't interfere with your hearing?"

"Okay, go ahead."

He cleared his throat and sipped his juice. "Marina and I were a regular thing until a few weeks ago. She claimed I was distracted, and she was right. So we ended it. Or I thought we did. The other night, I found out that I'd ended it and she'd paused it." He took a couple of bites of his breakfast then continued. "She comes from the same place I do. A little town outside Napoli. This was a connection between us. She's a nice girl. I won't speak evil of her. She took our thing more seriously than I did, and it didn't break as easily as I'd expected. I've spent the past few days making sure she understands. I don't want any crossover, or however you call it."

I sighed and put down my fork. "I'm going to be honest. I like you. And I love this breakfast. But if I end up believing you're telling me the whole truth, it'll be a conscious decision I'm making. And with my history, that decision takes some effort. I don't expect or want a commitment, but I don't like crossover, as you say."

"I don't either."

"And the questions thing? It bothers me."

"I can't negotiate that."

"Then what are we doing?"

"We are enjoying ourselves. Do you object to that?"

"I guess I can live with it for now. It'll come to bite us, though."

"Maybe." He leaned in to kiss me, much of his hardness and cocky arrogance gone. His lips looked soft and sweet as opposed to inaccessibly beautiful. His tongue was warm, slick, moving in harmony with his tender mouth. The smell of a pine forest in the morning, all dew and smoldering campfires, swelling my senses.

I wanted him. His neck, his jaw, his legs between mine. I wanted to suck on his fingers and thumbs. I reached between his legs, and he stopped me.

"This was only breakfast."

I groaned. "Please?"

"Tempting, Contessa. But it's been twice, and too hurried both times. The next time we fuck, it's going to be for a few hours, and you're going to need to be wheeled out. I'm not cheating you again." He reached for the dishes. "I'll clean up. Go get ready for work. I'll see you this weekend."

By the time I'd brushed my teeth and put my hair and makeup in order, he'd finished clearing the island. We walked out the door kissing. I didn't think I'd ever been so happy. Then I remembered what I'd promised Daniel, and by the time Antonio closed my car door and stepped away, my happiness had been worn away by the friction of reality.

I'd told Daniel it was over, and that had just changed, and I didn't even know how. I was curious about Antonio's alleged corruption. I couldn't be with a criminal, much less a murderer. Not since my first experience at thirteen, which left me scarred and the boy dead, had I encountered a dangerous man. I'd kept clear of all manner of worthless street punk—until Antonio, who could still back off any question he didn't feel like answering.

We were together. We weren't. It didn't matter. I was looking at those books.

Chapter 18.

My expertise was in accounting, but really, it was in the movement and flow of money. I looked at ledgers with a broad eye, finding patterns and flow. Like rivers on a map that fell into lakes, disappeared into mountains, and got spit into the ocean, the shifts of money were seen best from far away, with the finer details removed.

Bill and Phyllis, the core of the DA's financial analysts, were a married couple who had met in the Los Angeles district attorney's office forty-three years previous. They were detail people, in all their Midwestern glory—she was from Cadillac, Michigan and he was from Collett, Indiana. They reveled in getting it right, in not one shred of a detail falling through their fingers.

Thus, they missed everything.

If they'd understood the first law of fiscal dynamics—that money cannot be gained or lost, only moved—they'd understand that it all went somewhere. It was most important to follow a flow of cash downriver, and let the creeks taper into mysterious blue points. The answer was in the streams' and the rivers' undercurrents.

"Hi," I said.

"Hello, dear," Phyllis said, gracing me with a brilliant smile. "How are you?"

"Fine." I put my bag on the table.

Bill sat at the old banker's desk, tapping on a loud keyboard, his face a few inches too close to the screen. "Got mail from the boss." His chin pointed at his screen, eyes squinted. "Miss Drazen's looking at the Giraldi files. That right, Miss Drazen?"

"Theresa. Yes. If you don't mind?"

"We looked at them already. There's nothing there. We had the guys from downstairs working with us."

"Probably," I said. I didn't want to step on his toes, or the toes of the hundreds who had pored over the documents. "Just a new set of eyes."

"Have at it." He felt abused, if his expression was any indication. He dragged four document boxes from a shelf, one at a time, with the scratch of heavy cardboard sliding on wood.

"Anything digital?" I asked.

"Some," said Phyllis, opening the boxes. "I'll get it for you."

Bill wiped his nose with a cotton handkerchief, fidgeted, and sat. Poor guy. I'd flattened his toes, and it wasn't even lunchtime. I slid folders out, and with them came a scent. Not the musty odor of dust bunnies and paper residue. It was cologne, spicy and sweet with an undercurrent of pine trees after a rain. I caught a hint of something that I couldn't identify until I'd unloaded the whole box.

I inhaled again, trying to catch it, but it was gone. Only the dewy forest morning remained.

I hadn't spent more than an hour with the ledgers before I caught something. Just a few million in property tax payments. Legal payments from legal accounts containing legally obtained money.

One house in particular, in the center of the lots, had been purchased three years earlier with money from an international trust. The rest had been snapped up in the previous six months. It was a lot of property, tight together in the hills of Mount Washington, and it rankled.

Chapter 19.

Margie's red hair was tied back in a low ponytail, but strands had found their way free to drape over her cheeks. She was on her second chardonnay, and lunch hadn't even arrived. She could have had seven more and still litigated a murder trial.

"Mob lawyers are consigliore," she said. "They learn the law to get around it. But they don't get to be boss."

"Why not?"

"They're not made. Before you ask, made means protected. And other things. It's a whole freemason ceremonial shindig. They have to kill someone. Contract killing, not a vendetta. Now do I get to know why you're asking?"

"Because you'd know."

"Oh, shifty sister. Very shifty. You know what I meant." She waved as if swatting away murder. Then she nodded and sat up a little.

I followed her gaze to Jonathan, who sauntered toward us after shaking hands with the owner. He kissed Margie first, then me. A waiter put a scotch in front of him.

"Sorry, I'm late," he said.

"How was San Francisco?" Margie asked.

"Wet, cold, and amusingly liberal. I saw your picture in the paper," he said to me. "You're taking him back?"

"No."

"She has other things on her mind," Margie said.

"Such as?" He looked at me over the rim of his glass.

"Nothing."

"She's either writing a book or dating a mafia don," Margie said.

I went cold and hot at the same time. I set my face so it betrayed nothing. If Margie or Jonathan had suspected anything, they would have noticed the two percent change in my demeanor, but they only knew what I'd told them.

"Top secret," I said. "This doesn't leave the table. Drazen pledge."

"Pledge open," Margie said.

"Pledged," Jonathan agreed, holding up his hand lazily.

I dropped my voice. "Dan got some files on a certain crime organization from the NSA, and he's having me look at them."

Their reaction was immediate and definitive. Margie dropped her fork as if it was white hot. Jonathan picked up his whiskey glass, shaking his head.

"Is he trying to get you killed?" Jonathan asked.

"He needs to grow a set of fucking balls," Margie added.

She tilted her head a little, as if checking to see if I was going to make a fuss about her language. She'd once verbally cornered me at Thanksgiving dinner, bullying me into describing *why,* which I couldn't. Mom had begged her to stop, and Daddy had broken out laughing at my tears.

"Marge, really." Jonathan tapped his phone. "It's not that big a deal. He's the DA. If he can't protect her—"

But Margie continued undaunted. "Please, let me be the one to explain the obvious. If the mafia doesn't come after you for looking into their books, whoever's running against him will use you to undermine him. Think Hillary Clinton doing healthcare. Giving your disgraced ex-fiancé—"

"Thanks. I appreciate you defining me."

"The press will do a fine job without me," she said.

"Leave it to them then."

I glanced at my brother. He was fully engaged with his phone, smiling as if the Dodgers had won the Series. I knew he'd heard everything but had no intention of stepping into rescue me.

"Is he trying to get you back?" Margie asked. "This is his plan?"

"This was fun." Jonathan glanced up from his phone while still texting. "No, wait, we're in pledge. This wasn't fun at all."

Part of being "in pledge" was secrecy partnered with honesty, no matter how hurtful.

Jonathan put down his phone and leaned into me. "Most things, Dad can save you from, and he will."

"For a price," Margie muttered into her glass.

"Right," Jonathan continued. "But this? The mob? I don't know. That's big fish."

Our food arrived: sour lemon salads and more wine than anyone should drink at noon on a workday. We leaned back and let the waiter serve us, laying down oversized white plates and offering ground black pepper. Margie and Jonathan started eating, and I smoothed a crease in the tablecloth. Everything looked washed out by the sun and fill lights, every corner and curve of my body visible.

"We don't know if it's organized crime," I said. "Everything looks clean. Dan's looking for something illegal."

"I don't like it," Margie said.

"That's because you hate Daniel," I said.

"I was there. I saw what he did to you." Margie speared salad and glanced at me, head not moving, expression bland and open. Her lawyer look.

"I think I found something," I said. "But I'm not sure."

"Proceed quietly."

"I noticed some transactions. Real estate taxes. I followed the addresses to Mount Washington. The lots are grouped together in a really bad area. Fire sale prices."

Jonathan plopped his phone down and leaned back in his chair.

"You look like you just ate a canary," Margie said to him.

"I'm about to," he said. "Now, Margaret, stop bullying her. You're being bitter."

"Fuck you."

He turned to me. "Theresa, tell me about those buildings. Open permits? Zoning changes?"

"I don't know."

"Calls to the police about squatters? Still water?"

"I don't know."

"Complaints to Building and Safety?"

"Should I be making a list?"

He pushed his plate aside and put his elbows on the table. "If they're warehousing property, they'd raze the structures to get rid of the reporting problems. Then they'd just build an ugly apartment building when they had the land they needed. But they're keeping fire and liability traps standing. And that neighborhood... there's no way some kids won't use those buildings for business and burn the places down cooking meth."

"Who the fuck cares?" Margie moaned.

"Real estate fraud isn't covered under RICO, so they won't be federally prosecuted if they get caught doing whatever they're doing. You'd have mentioned that if you weren't busy giving her a hard fucking time."

"I'm trying to discourage her."

"Something's going on with those buildings, Theresa," he said. "Get your man to figure out what it is."

"Great idea." Margie put her napkin on the table and stood. "Encourage her. I'm going to the ladies'. By the time I get back, I expect bullets through the window."

We watched her stride across the room.

I sighed. "She thinks I'm made of sugar." I pushed my salad around my plate. Jonathan didn't say anything, and I didn't realize he was staring at me until I looked up.

"What's going on?" he asked as if he expected an answer. As if "nothing" wouldn't cut it.

We knew each other too well. As kids, the eight of us had had the option of banding together or falling apart. As a result, the youngest and the oldest had wound into two cliques, held together on the spool of Margie.

"Is this your way of getting him back?" Jonathan said. "Keeping an eye on him?"

The silence between us became long and tense, but he wouldn't give an inch. I thought Margie had gone to the bathroom in Peru.

"It's not that simple," I said.

"Go on."

"There's someone else. I won't talk about it more."

"Ah." He leaned back. "Use someone else as a threat, and then he tries to get you back with these books as an excuse? You're a tactician. I forgot to thank you for your suggestion to bring a woman I wasn't related to. Worked."

"Really? Jessica came back? That's amazing."

"Yes, but I don't want her. I'm keeping the new one. Unexpected upside."

I was stunned into silence. He'd let go of something he'd been holding onto for a long time. "What happened to change your mind?"

"It was just gone. Whatever was there. Poof, gone. And for a while, too. Which is great, but neither of them is going to get me killed. You? You're getting deep in shit."

I didn't want to say another word about it because I didn't want to spin out of control. I just wanted to find out about Antonio without asking him questions.

"You speak Italian, right?" I said.

"Yes."

He spoke everything. It was his gift.

"*Come vuoi tu.* What does that mean?"

"Kind of 'as you wish,' more or less. Why?"

"Pledge closed," I said.

"Fine. Pledge closed."

Margie came up behind us. "Closing pledge. Who wants coffee?"

Chapter 20.

Like every other part of central and eastern Los Angeles, Mount Washington was facing a real estate renaissance. Yet that particular hill seemed to have been passed over. The commercial district was a row of empty storefronts with gates pulled shut, broken glass, some burned out, and most graffitied over. Five blocks of third-world devastation stretched in either direction. I turned left up the hill, cracked asphalt bouncing my little car. The sidewalks ended under deep, thorny underbrush. Even at nine in the morning, I heard the beats of someone's music on the other side of the hill.

A right, then another left, and I found an eight-foot high chain-link fence stretched around a hairpin turn and up the hill. Across the street, another fence. The buildings were overgrown, unkempt, with peeling stucco and beams warped under the passion flower vines. When I opened my car door, an avocado with the squirrel-sized bite rolled down the hill with a *skit skit skoot*, popping up on a crack in the pavement and landing on the asphalt. I looked up. A cloud-high avocado tree shaded the block, spitting its bounty onto the sidewalk.

I shut the door. My car made a familiar chirp that alerted the neighborhood that something expensive was nearby. I glanced back at it then forward.

The late Frankie Giraldi had bought everything behind those fences, from what I could tell, but one house he'd bought first. He'd purchased it as an individual. Years later, his estate had moved it into trust and bought up everything around it.

The executor of the trust was the law firm of Mansiatti, Rowenstein, and Karo. Antonio Spinelli, Esq., LLP had bought them when they went belly up. They had one client: the Frank Giraldi estate. A snake eating itself. The estate's trust owned the property, and Antonio managed the trust. Did he actually own it outright? I couldn't tell from the papers I'd had in front of me.

The overgrowth detonated my allergies. I felt my sinuses swell and press against the bones of my face. A drip tickled the back of my nose. I checked my bag. Advil, tampons, wet wipes, and an empty tissue packet. Great. The tickle worked its way to the back of my throat. I put my hand in front of my mouth, checked to see if anyone was around, and made a very unladylike noise to scratch my throat as I walked down the block.

I found the house. I was allergic to just about everything growing around it.

I didn't know what I'd expected, but there was nothing but a run down, bright yellow house with a fifty-foot front yard. An old Fiat was parked on top of rosebush stumps. Stacks of faded children's toys pressed against the fence. Bars on the windows. A porch stacked with bags of leaves. The driveway had been kept clear though, which meant someone came in and out often enough to need a path. A few steps to the right, I saw muddy tire tracks from something bigger than a car.

The entrance to the drive had been chained shut. Though a hole had been cut in the fence at the next dilapidated house, it had been repaired with sharp twists of wire. I walked on a few feet and found a new opening.

I crawled through it. A thorny strand of brush found my stocking and gave it a good yank. I had an extra pair in the car, but I was still anxious about the drooping egg shape at my calf. Pushing past bamboo, bushes with sticky burrs, and tall weeds with yellow flowers that I knew tasted like broccoli, I came out into the end of the driveway, at the front end of the backyard.

The house had been built into a hill, so the backyard was at a slant, the square footage taken up by a slope that got more vertical as it bent away from the house. The structure itself was no surprise, with its beaten yellow paint and bent eaves. But the fence surprised me. Though the barriers from the street were old, hand-repaired chain link, the fences between the properties were new.

A loud crack echoed off the mountain. It could have been anything. A car backfiring. A piece of lumber snapping. Even a shotgun.

A smack of fear in my lower back sent me rushing through the bamboo and mustard weeds and through the hole in the fence, leaving behind strands of nylon for the thorns. I ran down the block and hurled myself at my car, almost twisting my ankle. The car blooped and I got in, turning the key before buckling. A drip of snot freed itself from my left sinus.

The car didn't start.

Daniel's voice bounced around my head, complaining that the car was unreliable, maintenance-heavy. He was right, and I was stuck on Mount Washington, turning my key repeatedly while nothing happened and a line of clear snot dropped down my lip.

My box of tissues was wedged under the passenger seat. Since I was stuck, and uncomfortable, and frustrated, I let go of the key and reached under the seat, rooting around for the feel of flat cardboard. I touched it and pushed, but a heavy iron pole got in the way. It was a security device called the Club that had been a big thing in the eighties, when the last owner had bought the car. Though I'd never used it, I kept it, even when it got in my damn way. I got the iron bar out and unbuckled my seatbelt. Leaning over, I curled my arm under the seat. The snot that had been sitting uncomfortably on my upper lip followed gravity. I shifted to get a look at what the box was caught on and yanked it free.

Clackclackclack

The sound of a ring rapping on the window. Too late to notice my skirt was hiked up, and I was showing full-on black garter belt to the world. I twisted to get a look at the guy standing over my car. He wore a neat striped shirt under a light windbreaker.

"You all right?" His voice was muffled through the glass.

I pulled my skirt down and sat up. "I'm fine." I snapped the last tissue out of the box and wiped my nose quickly. I cranked down the window.

"This is a nice car."

"Yeah, it won't move." I got a good look at him and recognized him by the bow lips. I held up a pointer finger and squinted, the universal sign for unreliable recognition.

"I thought I knew you," he said. "How's your sister?"

"Never better. Can you give me a push?"

"Sure. I know a garage down the street. They're honest."

There seemed to be red zones everywhere, so the garage was probably a good idea. "All right. I never got your name," I said.

"Paulie. Paulie Patalano."

"Nice to meet you again, Paulie."

Another man got out of a car behind me. He had a low forehead and moustache.

"This is Lorenzo. He's harmless," Paulie said.

"Hey, Paulie."

"Zo, this is Theresa. We're giving her a push to East Side. Yeah?"

Zo agreed. They pushed, joking the entire time about horsepower, the division of thrust between them, and who got to direct traffic when we crossed Marmion Way onto Figueroa. I steered and wondered at the odds of meeting the bow-lipped man again. When one considered the actual mathematical odds, chance meetings were nearly impossible, yet they happened all the time.

And then, I wondered, what were the odds that Antonio was somewhere near his friend? Was he somehow behind any of this?

East Side Motors appeared a block away. A typical car repair dump, with a dirty yellow and black sign advertising that every car brand in the universe was a specialty, it looked no better than any other shop around. As we got closer, it became apparent that business was brisk. The lot was packed, and men in grey jumpsuits hustled around bumpers and grilles, moving cars, shouting, and laughing.

I turned in and was greeted by a balding guy with a chambray shirt and moustache. He opened the door as soon as I stopped.

"Ma'am," he said, "we don't do German cars."

I looked up at the sign. What had looked like every brand in the universe was actually every brand in Italy. A quick glance around the lot revealed Maseratis, Ferraris, Alpha Romeos, but no German, Japanese, or American cars.

"It won't turn over," I said. "Could you hold it until I get a tow? I'll pay for the storage."

"You got it." He turned to Paulie. "Sir? Are we charging?"

"No fucking way. She keeps it here as long as she needs to." He held his hand to me. "Come on to the back."

His manner was so friendly and professional, I thought nothing of following him. I thought I'd find coffee, a seat, a stale donut perhaps. But as I walked through the hustle of the lot into the dim garage, where everything looked dusted with grime, a man in a clean, dark yellow sweater and grey jacket looked up into the underbelly of an old Ducati, exposing the tautness of his throat. Such a vulnerable position, yet he held it with supreme confidence. Antonio. Another chance meeting that I was beginning to think had little to do with the natural laws of probability.

"Spin," called Paulie from behind me.

When Antonio pulled his arms down from the Ducati, he saw me and seemed as surprised at my presence. I kept doing probabilities in my head, switching the numbers between him knowing and not knowing.

"Contessa?" he said, glancing at me then his friend.

"Up by *l'uovo*," Paulie said.

A concerned look crossed Antonio's face, but then it was gone with a nod and a smile. He snapped a handkerchief from his pocket and carefully wiped the engine grease off his fingers. Having erased reactions from my face my whole life, I knew exactly what he was doing. He was collecting himself from surprise.

"I got this, Pauls."

"Oh yeah?"

"Yeah. We'll be in the office," Antonio said.

They stared at each other for a moment, then Paulie held out his hand. They shook on it.

"Benny!" Antonio called to a stocky man tapping at a smudged keyboard. "Friction plates, rubber, and rings, okay?"

"You got it, boss."

Boss? Okay. Lawyer. Restaurateur. Mechanic.

"Come on." He held out his hand for me.

I didn't take it. I trusted him less and less as the minutes wore on. Antonio just turned and walked through a door, holding it open as he passed into a clean, sundrenched room with industrial grey carpet and car posters.

I followed him. Coffee had been set up for the people waiting and reading magazines. Behind a counter with phone banks and more magazines sat a woman in her fifties.

"Spin," she said in a thick Italian accent, handing him a clipboard. "Sign please. I want to order the paint."

He signed without looking and walked to another door marked "Private."

I stopped. "I'm surprised to see you."

"I have the same feeling."

The middle-aged woman went about her business as if nothing was happening.

"You could have called if you wanted to see me," he continued.

"I didn't come to see you." With those words, I realized the trouble I was in. I'd been asking questions behind his back. Investigating. I couldn't imagine how angry he would be. I had no reason to be in that neighborhood except to stare at a bunch of innocently acquired property that was just a cluster of buildings with zero illegal activity surrounding them. Maybe that was my secret weapon.

"Really?" he said with a raised brow.

I smiled coyly. "I'm here now."

He opened the door and smiled back, but I couldn't tell if he'd fallen for my act or not. The office was walled in glass and striped with shadows from natural wood blinds. The décor was warmer than the rest of the business, with a dark wood desk with clawfoot legs, shelves with car manuals, and a buffed matte wood floor. Antonio closed the blinds, and my eyes adjusted. The diffused light was still more than enough to see by.

"So," he said, "up by the yellow house?"

"There was a yellow house. Needs a paint job."

He nodded. "It's not for sale."

"I hoped the owner would be in. Maybe I could talk him into selling."

"You couldn't afford it." He took two steps forward and was right in front of me.

"I have lots of money," I whispered.

"He isn't interested in your money."

His lips were on mine before he'd even completed the last vowel. His tongue found my tongue, and his hands were under my shirt, caressing my ribs, slipping under my bra. He believed it. He believed I'd come to the neighborhood hoping to see him. Maybe there was a sliver of truth to that. My legs wrapped around him, and he put his hand up my skirt unceremoniously.

He pressed his hips into the thin lace of my underwear. Would he rip another pair? I hoped so. From the bottom of my pelvis, I hoped he would.

"I don't have hours to fuck you like you deserve." He slipped a finger under my panties, finding where I was wettest. "I have a few minutes to make you hold back a scream."

He found my engorged clit, and I stiffened. He pushed me onto the arm of a chair. My arms braced me as his hand stroked.

"How did you come here, Theresa?" he said as his fingertips blinded me with sensations, making me vulnerable.

I couldn't think. "The one ten freeway."

He pulled away, moving his hand so his thumb rotated on my clit as he stood over me. I felt intimidated and powerless, and I was as afraid as I was aroused.

"Look at me," he whispered tenderly. "Spread your legs."

I did it, looking and spreading until both hurt.

He was perfectly put together, with one hand in me the way it had just been inside a transmission. "What were you doing by the yellow house?"

"I wanted to see where you lived."

"That's not my legal address."

"I hope not. It was a mess."

He answered my sarcasm by sliding two fingers into my soaking hole. "I didn't get a call about anyone trespassing at my house."

"Oh God, Antonio, I'm so close."

I noticed, as I got closer, that he wasn't telling me what he was going to do to me. Where was the dirty talk? Something was wrong, but I was too close to the incoming tide of my sexual pleasure to think clearly about what that meant.

He put his hand on the back of the chair and leaned down, his strokes getting lighter and softer, keeping me on the edge. "I want to like you, Contessa. I want to. But I can't trust you."

His words didn't sink in soon enough. My wet, engorged sex was still in his hand. On the third stroke, I exploded in an orgasm that was supposed to be a release, but instead was humiliating. The emotional disconnect cut the pleasure short, and I twisted away from him, breathing heavily with my bra half pulled over my breasts and my skirt bunched at my waist.

"What was that?" I said.

"I wondered how you just show up in my neighborhood." He took the grease-smeared hankie from his pocket and wiped the fingers that had been inside me. "You weren't looking for my house. You were looking for *something*. The district attorney sent you. You've been working for him the whole time, haven't you? It's on the side of a barn, like you say."

"You think my ex sent me to fuck you?" I straightened my clothes, seething so hard I didn't even care what I said or how I said it. But the more I wanted to say what was on my mind, the more crowded my mind became. "You think he's whoring me out? What kind of world do you live in? And let me assure you, the lack of trust is mutual. Talk about what's on the side of a barn. You react to questions like I'm spraying acid on you. You have no real law practice. A hundred different businesses. You can bust a guy's face on the hood of a car. Maybe the police questioned you so many times because you're a criminal lowlife."

I brushed past him, but he caught my upper arm. "Let go of me," I growled from deep in my throat.

"I run legitimate businesses."

"What better way to do the laundry?"

His tongue pressed between his lips, and his eyes drifted to my mouth in a nanosecond of weakness. "Be careful."

"Good advice. I'm staying away from the dirtbags from now on."

He tightened his grip on my arm, and we stood like that, breathing each other's air, until a light rap came from the other side of the door.

"Spin?"

He waited a second and kept his eyes on mine as he answered. "Yeah, Zo?"

"Tow's here, and they don't know where to take the Beemer."

Silence hung between us. His jaw moved as if he was grinding his teeth. I held his gaze. He could go straight to hell, and I still wanted him. The knock came again.

Antonio whipped his head around and shouted, "What!"

Zo's voice was timid. "The tow guy has another call."

Antonio pulled me to him so hard I knew I would walk out of there with a nice bruise. He pressed his lips together as if he had something to say but didn't know how to say it.

I answered as if he'd spoken. "I know what's between us. I know it's real, as real as anything I've ever felt for a man. And I know you don't really believe Daniel whored me out to get information. Even if you think he'd do something like that, you know in your heart I wouldn't. But none of that matters. Even though you don't believe I have ulterior motives, you're scared of it." He loosened his grip just a little, and I took that as my cue to continue. "That's not the way to be together. It's too long a bridge to cross. Let's both be grown-ups and walk away before this gets uglier."

It took a few seconds, or forever, for him to remove his hand, his fingers slipping over my sleeve as if magnetized. I took a long breath, memorizing his scent, the thickness of his hair, the cleft in his jaw, the angle I held my head to look into his deep brown eyes.

"I'll have someone drive you home," he said.

"I can get a cab."

"I know. But someone from here will drive you." He opened the door.

Zo was right behind it, hunched and tense.

"Make sure she gets home," Antonio said.

"Sure, boss."

I followed Lorenzo and looked back for the briefest second, enough to catch Antonio closing the office door.

On the way out, I saw a man with a comb-over I would have sworn I recognized. He wasn't wearing a mechanic's jumpsuit, but a zipper jacket. His left eye was badly bruised, almost swelled shut, and a bandage held a cut together at his brow. It was Vito, and when he saw me, he turned and walked in the other direction.

After some discussion, some signed papers, a few minutes spent waiting for something I couldn't remember because I was distracted by Antonio's presence in his office and the distance between us, I let Paulie Patalano drive me home. Apparently, my house was on his way.

Chapter 21.

"You ever been in a Ferrari?" Paulie asked.

"You're joking," I said as I got into the flashy yellow car.

"Gotta ask." He slid into the driver's side and shifted his shoulder a little, touching something behind him before he got his seatbelt on.

I'd dated a detective in college, and he made the same exact move when he got into a car. When he'd caught me watching, I got a lecture about how he had to wear his gun even when off-duty and how he didn't want to take it off for a short drive. We had a long drive ahead of us, and poor Paulie was going to be very uncomfortable. He put the top down, and we got onto the freeway.

"Thanks for driving," I said once we hit traffic and the wind didn't whip as much.

"I was heading out this way." He drove with the seat pushed all the way back and his wrist on the top of the wheel.

I had my bag in my lap and my knees pressed together. "I'm glad you found me at the bottom of that hill."

"Yeah."

"You work at the car shop?"

He smiled. Changed lanes. Adjusted the hunk of metal at his back. "I own it with Spin."

"Oh, partners?"

"In everything. He's like my brother. Pisses off my real brothers, but they're douchebags. A cop and a lawyer."

"And you?"

"Businessman."

I put on my most political comportment because it was obvious what kind of business he did from the back of a body shop, with loose hours, carrying a firearm. I'd never seen one on Antonio though, which seemed strange.

I didn't care. No, I shouldn't care. It should all be meaningless small talk in a yellow Ferrari going twenty miles per hour on the 10 freeway.

"You weren't really heading west, were you?" I said more as a statement than a question.

"Zo is the only other guy I'd trust to not speed, and he'd bore the paint off the car." He glanced at me. "We just fixed it. He'd return it with primer, shrugging like, 'dunno what happened, boss, I was just talking.'"

I laughed. "Sure."

"And, you know, I want to get to know you. See what your deal is."

Did he think I was working for the DA as well? I couldn't easily ask. "My deal?"

"Spin likes you. Ain't no secret."

The road opened up for absolutely no reason, and the wind whipped my hair like cotton candy.

"I'm sure he likes plenty of girls." I pulled out my bun and let my hair fly.

"Not like this," Paulie said.

"Like what?"

He shook his head and put his eyes on the road.

"No, really," I said. "I'm not asking you to tell stories about your friend."

"Oh no? You women, you're all alike."

"Like what?"

"Like you don't want a guy to like you. You have to know how much. How high. How deep. Never simple. So before you ask again, he's never looked at a woman who's not from home."

"Pretty small dating pool."

"He don't date. You ain't getting another word outta me." He raised his index finger and put it to his lips. "Just know I'll protect him with my life."

"He's a lucky guy."

"Right about that."

Nothing he said should have hurt me, because my thing with Antonio was done, but as I watched the city blow by me, it did.

***

Katrina was on set when I got home. The loft had never seemed so big, so modern, so clean. Everything had a place, and everything was in it. The surfaces were wiped sterile, and dust bunnies were eradicated.

I threw my bag on the couch. It didn't belong there, but I left it.

I missed something. I felt a longing and a regret for something I'd lost. I couldn't pin it down. In a way, it was Daniel. I missed his constant talking on the phone, the hum of his ambition, the steady foursquare geometry of his dependence. I missed his presence spreading over me even when he traveled, covering me in a way Katrina's couldn't.

"Fuck you, Daniel," I whispered. I threw my jacket over a chair and left it.

Dad had always said all we'd ever need was our family, and I'd never doubted him. But he was wrong. Dead wrong. I couldn't mold my life into any of my sisters'. I couldn't take joy in breathing their air, or feel the electricity of physical connection. I couldn't look at my house and see them coexisting with me as anything but an imposition.

The refrigerator. Vegetables in the crisper. Proteins on the bottom shelf. Leftovers above that, and on the top, condiments. I pulled out a tub of hummus. Crackers on the bottom shelf two over from the sink. I stood at the island, dipping, eating, dipping, eating. Double-dipping, even.

A blob of hummus plopped onto the counter. I swiped it up and ate it. The residual paste was the only disruption of the pristine surface.

What the hell had happened with Antonio? What was I thinking? Had I been trying to get away from Daniel in the most violent way possible? Was I trying to reject not just my comfort zone, but my lawfulness? Wasn't there an easier way to do that than by getting involved with someone I had nothing in common with? No matter how my body reacted to him. No matter how excited or how free he made me feel. No matter how alive I felt around him.

But I couldn't shake the sense of profound regret. I'd dodged a bullet but fallen onto a knife.

I let the paper towel roll drop from my hand. It rolled from the kitchen island to the front door. I needed something in my life besides a job and a man. I needed a purpose. I had nothing to care about besides myself. No wonder Daniel's infidelity had thrown me so far off the deep end.

I whipped the stepstool around to the refrigerator and reached into the cabinet above it. As a kid, I'd collected porcelain swans. I didn't know why, but I loved swans. Their grace, their delicacy. But when we moved to the loft, the mismatched animals didn't make sense, so I hid them in the highest cabinet, where they wouldn't get broken.

I took the first one out. It had a blue ribbon that flew in the wind as it raised its wings to take flight. It had cost a shameful amount. I put it on the counter. The next one was Lladro. Cheap, with a little cupid. There was a black one. An ugly duckling. One with an apron. Laughing. Swimming. Necks twisted together. I put them all on the counter until I came to the little white one in the back.

It was made of Legos. It had a red collar in flattish bricks and a bright yellow beak. My nephew David had made it for me some random Christmas. Hyper and brilliant David. How old had he been? Four? Aunt Theresa loved swans, and he'd made her a bird with such care. And she'd put it in the back of a cabinet she couldn't even reach because it didn't go with the décor.

"Fuck you, Aunt Theresa." I got down from the stepstool and put the Lego swan in the center of the island.

I opened my dish cabinet. I loved my dishes. They had blue stars with gold flourishes. Why were they in a cabinet? I took them out and laid them on the counter in piles that specifically made no sense. My flatware had been chosen with utmost care. With no room on the counter, I threw the silver on the floor like pick-up sticks.

All of it came out. Everything in the cabinets I'd ever chosen. Everything I liked. Everything beautiful and worthy. The glass jelly jars and inherited Depression glass. The gold-leaf embellished glass rack from my great-grandmother. I didn't break anything, but the frosted glass tray we got as an engagement gift almost slipped off the sink. I caught it and continued. Out of style napkin holders. Stained plastic containers. A red sippy cup Sheila had left behind on some visit. Out out out.

When I got to the last cabinet and found the dust and dirt in the back of it, I stepped into the living room where I could see the open kitchen. It was a wreck. I'd left all the cabinet doors open, and nothing was neatly or safely placed.

I reached over the island and moved some stacks until I found the little Lego swan. I had a date with my empty bed. I could figure out what to do with my life in the morning.

The bed still seemed too big. The mess downstairs offered a momentary peace then irked me into wakefulness. But I refused to go down and clean it. I had put my Lego swan on the nightstand, and when I wondered if I should just go put my life back in the cabinets, the swan clearly said no. Go to sleep. Think about the mess tomorrow.

Katrina came in. Lights went on. The TV went on. The toilet flushed. The water ran. The TV went off. The lights went off. I slept.

Chapter 22.

"What happened?" Katrina asked as she pulled a swan-shaped coffee cup from the pile. Its neck was a handle, and its wings wrapped around the bowl. "I can't find the spoons."

I picked one up from the floor. "Here. I'll wash it."

She snatched it and blew on it. "Sanitizing pixie dust. Knife too, please."

I picked one of my best silver butter knives off the floor and handed it to her without offering to wash it. The sink was full of china cruets anyway.

"I'll put it all away later."

"Whatever." She cleared a space in front of the coffee pot and poured herself some.

"But we have to be on set today, then I have work on Monday. I'll get Manuela on it when she comes Tuesday," I said.

"Whatever."

"Are you mad?"

"Mad? No. I almost broke all these damned dishes last night in a rage, but not because of them. Only because they were in front of me."

I handed her a dish. "Go ahead. Break it."

She took it and waved it up and down, balancing it on her fingertips like half a seesaw. Then she put it on top of its stack. "It's pointless." She put the heels of her hands to her eyes and growled in a tantrum.

"What?"

"Apogee fell through," she shouted, as if yelling at the entire Hollywood system.

"What? They won't distribute it?"

"No, they backed out of post-production."

"Why?"

"Because." She shook her hands as if she was at a loss for words. "Lenny Garsh moved to Ultimate, and the new guy's only backing projects he believes in. Completed projects." She stamped her feet. Full-on tantrum. "Fuck fuck fuck fuck. I have the editing bay and ADR place booked, and I can't pay."

"Okay, we can work this out."

"There's nothing to work out. I'm screwed. I tapped everyone I know to do production. Now there's no point in even finishing." Her face collapsed. It took seconds for the muscles to go slack and the tears to gather. She sniffed, hard and wet. "Fuck, what am I going to tell Michael? He was depending on this. He's a star, you know? In his gut. And I told him... I told him we'd get this done."

"You will get this done," I said, taking her shoulders.

"Ernie shot it free because he believed in me."

"Katrina—"

"It's my job to get the money, and I let everyone down." She was full-on blubbering and trying to talk through hitching gasps.

I put my arms around her. "Directrix?"

I was answered with sobs.

"You have another week of production. Do you have the money to finish it?"

She nodded into my shoulder. "But—"

"No buts. Get it together."

"I don't have enough. I missed a wide on the dinner scene."

"You won't be the first. Now we have twenty minutes to get out of here and get to set. People are waiting."

She pulled away and wiped her eyes. "I have to tell them."

"No." I put up my hands. "What is wrong with you? That'll kill the momentum."

She put her head in her hands. "I don't know what I'm thinking."

"Go take a shower, and let's go. Come on. I took a week off work to finish this with you. We have to get this thing in the can by Friday. Reschedule your ADR. It's a phone call, right?"

"If they have space. They book months in advance."

"Fast, cheap, or good," I said, quoting the old filmmaking motto that no one can get more than two of the three. "Fast isn't happening."

"I have to eat. I can't mooch off you forever."

"Whatever. Let's deal with today. Okay? We're shooting at the café again?"

"Yes."

"If you start freaking out, you come to me, right?"

"I love you, Tee Dray. You're so together."

Chapter 23.

I checked my phone after the thirty-fifth take. It was a long shot of Michael watching the woman in question over the food counter, and with so many moving parts, it was difficult to get. But the shot was meant to show infinite hours of longing for a woman who didn't want him, and on the thirty-sixth try, it was stunning.

I didn't expect Antonio to try to reach me, but I was surprised by my burning hope. Did I want him? Or did I want him to want me? He was toxic, and I shouldn't touch him even if I was operating on all emotional cylinders, which I wasn't. I had to keep in the front of my mind the fact that I couldn't trust any man with my body or heart. No matter how intense. No matter how strong. No matter how much the sex was unlike anything I'd ever experienced.

Even thinking about Antonio, I felt a familiar throb between my legs. Even as I noted the placement of every extra's arms and legs, I ached for that treacherous man, his pine scent, his rock of a dick.

"Cut!"

Katrina was barely finished her encouragements to the actors before I had my phone out. Nothing from Antonio. Three from Gerry, Daniel's strategist. I got back to business making my notes. I needed to arrange my finances so I could get Katrina half a million dollars in such a way that she would accept it.

I didn't know how I'd get it done in time. I had a week before she lost her mind. I was incorporated, but not as an investor. I couldn't decide if I wanted her to know it was me who was fronting the money. It was two in the morning, and I was tired. Hardly ready for Gerry to show up in a three-piece suit looking as though he'd just woken up, showered, shaved, and taken his vitamins.

"Almost the first lady of the city," he said with a jovial tone, "packing binders in a parking lot."

"What are you doing here?" I stuffed the last of the day's work into a duffel.

"Los Angeles never sleeps."

"Daniel Brower does. A good five hours between midnight and dawn."

"That's when I get to work. Can we talk?"

I slung the bag over my shoulder. Katrina would get home on her own. "Sure. You're driving though. My car's busted."

***

The front seat of Gerry's Caddy SUV was bigger than the couch in my first apartment. The bag was in the back like a dead body.

"He's not performing," Gerry said, turning onto the 110. "Every time he flubs or goes back to some old habit, it's like a snowball. It hasn't affected his polling yet, but soon, it's gonna get obvious."

"After the election, he'll get it together again."

"He started biting his nails."

"The ring finger?"

"Yeah. In a meeting with Harold Genter. I think I bruised his calf."

I sighed. Years, I'd spent years in media skills sessions. We'd discussed that every movement, every breath, was ten times bigger on camera, and those moves flowed into real life. People wanted their leaders polished. Policy was secondary, and politics took third rung. If he was seen biting his nails, flipping his hair, or slouching, he'd be a laughingstock.

"He needs you," Gerry said.

"He should have thought of that."

"Okay, lady, yes. You can be bitter and aggrieved. You earned it. You happy? Are you going to hold your bag of self-righteousness into your dotage? It gets heavy when you get old. Believe me."

"I can't trust him ever again. How am I supposed to carry that around? And for how long? Into the presidency?"

"As long as you want." He drove on the surface streets— stop start stop start—obeying the lights even though no one was around.

I knew I'd let it go eventually. I'd learn to trust another man. He wouldn't be Daniel, of course. I would have to invest in someone else all over again. Get hurt, move on. Hurt someone, move on. Antonio had proven how easy that was. One day, I'd fall in love. Maybe. I was thirty-four. I'd never felt too late until Gerry asked about my dotage.

"I hurt all over," I said. "All the time. I don't know what I feel any more. I don't know what I want. I feel separate from my own thoughts. The fact that I'm telling this to a political strategist is enough of a red flag that I need to be medicated or institutionalized."

I didn't say that I think about hurting but not killing myself. I couldn't cry. I felt unanchored. I loved Daniel still. The last time I'd felt marginally alive was with Antonio. I'd always depended on men for my happiness.

"*Big Girls* is opening Friday," Gerry said as he pulled up in front of my building.

"Yeah."

"It's about domestic violence. We pitched that as your hot button during the campaign. I've seen the picture. It's good."

"You're making a movie recommendation?" I asked.

"Daniel is making it a point to see it and release a statement after."

"You're trying to set me up on a date? Are you serious?"

"This is a high stakes date, Theresa. Please."

I opened the car door and stepped out, slamming it shut and opening the back for my bag. "You're a crappy Cupid."

spin

I should have taken a cab.

***

Fucking Gerry. I walked in the door cursing him, flinging my bag into a corner.

Fucking fucking Gerry. The man was made of the finest, most indestructible plastic in the universe. He didn't have a feeling in him.

Or maybe he did. Maybe he just didn't have a feeling for me.

Or maybe he did. Maybe I didn't have a feeling for me.

Or maybe it wasn't about me. Maybe it was about Daniel and the city of Los Angeles. Maybe it was about a campaign I'd invested my heart and soul in, and when Daniel fell through, what I'd wanted for myself fell through.

Or maybe it didn't matter what Gerry thought was important. Maybe something was bothering me. Something that had excited me, given me something to look forward to, made me forget how much I despised my fucking life.

Antonio had made me feel alive, as if I'd been asleep for months. He shook me, slapped me. I was finally ready, and I'd thrown it away. It had been a casual nothing, a little dirty talk, something to fill the hours while I waited to get over Daniel. I wasn't allowed to get upset over such a little nothing, but I was desperately upset, and I couldn't admit it to myself until I was asked to be Daniel's beard yet again.

I picked up a porcelain swan by the neck. I knew what I was going to do before I did, and once decided, the tension released.

I smacked it against the edge of the table. It bounced. I smacked it harder. The body broke off, clacking to the ground, and I was left holding the tiny head. In seconds, the tension came back. It was only relieved when I looked at all of my swans and stopped caring whether they ever went back into the cabinet.

I didn't feel rage when I smashed the swans. I must have looked angry and emotional, but I wasn't. I was dead, empty, frozen, doing a job I'd contracted myself to do. I bashed them against the marble countertop, leaving millions of plaster, porcelain, and glass shards everywhere.

It took about seven minutes to destroy years' worth of swans and a few dishes. I stood over the puddle of sharp dust and said what I'd been too upset to consider.

"I want you."

I pushed a china blue swan wing to the right. It had separated from the rest of the swan but hadn't broken completely. Not nearly enough.

"I want you, you criminal punk."

I picked up my foot and smashed the wing under my heel.

"And I'm going to have you."

Chapter 24.

I paid my cleaning lady extra to make sense of the mess, sweep up the porcelain swan guts, and put everything back. I dressed for work before I called Antonio. No answer.

I texted.

> —*Call me, please. I want to discuss something with you*—

I read it over. It seemed very businesslike. I was a well-mannered person, but that didn't mean I had to evade everything, did it?

> —*Specifically, your cock*—

I smiled. That should do it.

***

I practically jumped out of bed the next morning. I layered slacks and a tight button-down shirt over a satin demi and lace panties. Rippable lace, because I was going to find that fucker and tell him what I thought, what I wanted, and how I wanted it. He would learn to trust me if I had to give him a signed affidavit and a blood sample.

I heard Katrina downstairs just as I was deciding to leave my hair down. No, I didn't hear Katrina—I heard a dish clatter along the concrete floor as if it had been kicked.

"Sorry!" I called as I ran down.

She blew on a dish and returned it to the pile. "What the fuck?" She pointed to my broken swans.

"You don't like the mess? I spent eight minutes making it."

She waved and pulled the coffee down then dropped it. "I don't care about the mess. It's you breaking things. You're Tee Dray. You don't break things."

As she scooped the coffee, I saw her hand shaking.

"Directrix," I said, "have some chamomile, please. You're jacked up."

"We're almost done. I'm excited. You coming to the wrap party?"

"I'm springing for an open bar."

Katrina flicked on the TV. The talking heads talked, and the news ticker ticked.

"You should bring the hot Italian," she said, reminding me of my text.

I checked my pocket. No response. "I might. The last time I saw him, it was weird."

"You didn't tell me."

"You're busy."

"So what happened?"

My lips stayed closed. I focused on the way they touched, because I had to shut up. It was just that kind of casual sharing and speculation that worried Antonio, and with good reason. I wanted to earn his trust behind his back.

"I think it's over," I said to deflect further questioning.

"Probably for the best. You know southern Europeans. They have a Madonna- whore complex. They either debase you and kick you to the curb, or revere you and never fuck you."

Again, I pressed my lips together to keep from speaking. He'd fucked me, and fucked me dirty. I felt a familiar tingle between my legs just remembering it. But he didn't want me to know about his life. It seemed as though he had disappeared long enough to get horny and then relentlessly pursue me when he wanted a whore. I hadn't noticed the pattern because I'd been so close to it.

I shook it off. I didn't have time to worry about how I was seen or wonder what he thought. I had to do what I wanted, and I wanted to feel alive again. He was like my drug, and I would either get a hit or go into withdrawal, but I wouldn't abdicate my right to chase him.

I checked my phone again. Nothing. Just a traffic alert. The 10 was jammed up because of a car-to-car shootout that had resulted in a five-car pileup and police actions across a mile-long stretch. Venice Boulevard was in the red from the overflow.

"Fuck," Katrina said.

"Yeah, the 10," I replied, but Katrina was looking at the TV.

"This has been going on for days already."

I looked over her shoulder. I recognized LaBrea Ave. The shot was daytime, and the tag said yesterday.

Two days of gang violence across the west side. Two shootings, one death in a seemingly unmotivated spree.

Daniel's face filled the screen. The signage in the background told me the news crew had caught him at a campaign rally. "We're working closely with the police to make sure justice is served."

They cut him off there. God help him if that was the meat of the interview.

Could this be Antonio? Somehow? If he was what Daniel said he was, then he certainly could be involved, but there were hundreds of gangs in the city. The victims didn't seem related, and the violence wasn't all deadly. There was speculation about Compton gangs, the SGV Angels, and an Armenian outfit in East Hollywood.

"Good thing we're downtown," Katrina said, turning away from the TV. "But everyone on the west side's going to miss call time."

Daniel appeared again, mouthing the same promises. His hand appeared on the screen. The right ring fingernail was bitten down.

Chapter 25.

I'd learned when a script supervisor was needed and when she'd spend hours waiting around, so I knew when I could split for an hour or two. My first stop was the garage in Mount Washington.

I got in my car, which had been quickly repaired once the ignition coil had been reconnected. My mechanic had shrugged. Old car. Things bend and tighten. It happens, apparently. I asked if someone could have done it on purpose, and he said something noncommittal, like "Anyone can do anything on purpose."

Especially when they wonder if you're snooping around.

I got to Antonio's repair shop in record time. A chest-constricting worry nearly kept me from driving in. The hum of activity I'd noticed last time was gone. The lot held half as many cars, and I didn't see as many guys in jumpsuits. When I got past the gate, no one greeted me. I parked and went into the office.

"Hi," I said to the woman behind the desk. "I'm looking for Antonio."

"He's out. You can just pull into the garage." She was new, her black hair down and gum cracking against her molars. She had an accent. Italian, again. She was older, but I couldn't help wonder if he'd fucked her.

"I was hoping to see him."

"Not in." She shuffled some papers.

"Any idea where he is?"

She regarded me seriously for the first time. "No. You can leave a message."

I thought about it for a second then declined. I texted him again.

—I still want to talk to you—

I didn't expect to hear back, and I didn't. I shot back downtown to finish the day's work.

***

Every time my phone dinged and buzzed, I hoped it was Antonio. But it was always Pam with some new meeting or appointment. I started seeing the world through the hopeful window of my device.

"Hey."

I spun around to find the source of the voice.

Michael stood behind me in costume: Dirty jeans. Grey T-shirt. A filthy apron and hair net. "We got a place from ReVal for the wrap party on Saturday. Some corporate loft they haven't staged yet."

"Wow. Nice work. Are we starting filming?"

"Nah, they're still getting the lights up."

I stepped deeper into the parking lot. "That getup really works for you."

Anything would work for him. He was a celebrity waiting to happen.

"Like it?" He pointed to a particularly egregious brown smear. "I had this chocolate streak put on just so people would think it was shit."

"Bold."

"That's my middle name. Speaking of—well, no, not speaking of. This is actually a major non sequitur."

We walked through the lot, ignored in the busy hustle of the camera crew testing every corner for the right light, adjusting scrims and lamps.

"I like a good non sequitur as much as the next person."

He stopped and turned toward me. "I heard we lost our post funding."

"You know Hollywood gossip is cheap."

"My agent told me."

"And agent gossip is the cheapest. Seriously, Michael, consider the source. Pilot season's happening when you'll be doing scene pickups for Katrina. He can't like that."

"You're not denying it."

"You assume I know in the first place."

"Still not denying it. You're an artist at that, you know." His smile seemed genuine, but it could have been acting. "Now, Ms. Ip? Not such an artist."

He took out a pack of cigarettes and poked one out. I was reminded of Antonio Spinelli's fluid motions, his clacking lighter, the smoke framing his face. Michael was less intense. My observations could have been colored by my sexual indifference. Sometimes, between two people who shared so little heat, a cigarette was just a cigarette.

"I'm glad you brought it up with Katrina first," I said. "She needs to know if something like this is going around town."

"I've done some of my best work in the past couple of weeks. Pilot season's not my future. This movie is."

"I'm glad you—"

"I do feel that way. Let me finish. If this film gets shelved, I'm shelved. I'm home in Park Forest, Illinois, working in the pizza shop on Blackhawk Way. I have no money to put up, but I would, and she knows that."

"Stop." When he tried to blow through me again, I held up my hand. "She won't take money from me."

"I know."

"You think you know a little too much."

"We haven't even scratched the surface." He took a scrap of paper from his apron pocket just as Ricky, the new AD, called talent to the set. "This guy funds low-budget, non-union gigs that run out of money."

I looked at the paper, though I suspected I knew the name already. Scott Mabat, Hollywood loan shark and part-time pornography producer. "This guy's a career-killer."

"He made Thomas Brandy who he is."

"A statistical anomaly. The rest couldn't pay him back and wound up in a ditch."

He stepped back toward set, where I also belonged. "I believe in this picture."

With that, he spun around and trotted inside, leaving behind the implication that I didn't. As I followed, I counted the days I had left to get Katrina her money.

***

When the set broke, I hopped over to the Spanish house in the hills. The gate was locked, and the driveway was empty. I got out and listened. No banging or hammering. No sledgehammer demolition on an ill-placed wall. Nothing but the screech of crickets.

I got back in the car. *Where to, Contessa?*

It had been four days. Was the trail getting cold, or was I just getting really crappy at this? I still had no idea where he lived. The car place was probably closed for the day. Where else had I seen him? Frontage. The offices of WDE. A Catholic Charities fundraiser. Katrina's set downtown, where he'd brought dinner and wine.

Zia.

I tapped my phone a few times and came up with a restaurant in Rancho Palos Verdes. A thirty-minute drive if the freeways had cleared from the spate of violence that had something or nothing at all to do with Antonio.

Chapter 26.

Zia's didn't look authentic. It looked like what authentic was supposed to look like. If you went to Italy, you'd expect every café and restaurant to have a supply of red checked tablecloths, containers of parmesan, and baskets of bread with saucers of butter. Considering the quality of the neighborhood and the sophistication of the residents, the cheesy décor was bound to be a turnoff.

I parked in the little lot and went around to the front, where two tables sat on the sidewalk. At one sat two men in their sixties, hunched over a game of dominoes. The one farthest, with the white moustache and huge belly, glanced at me, nodded, and rolled the dice. The other, in a fedora and open-necked shirt, didn't acknowledge me. A sense of apprehension came over me. I was stepping into Antonio's territory. Wasn't that exactly what he didn't want?

A wood bar stretched over one side of the restaurant, and the rest of the floor was taken up by small round tables and booths decorated with gingham and little oil and vinegar carts. A mural of Mount Vesuvius took up all available wall space.

Half of the four booths had little "reserved" tags on them, and at the other two sat clusters of men. One of them, a short guy with a brown shirt and goatee, stood between the two tables, speaking Italian as if he was regaling them with a story. He checked me out when I entered then went back to waving his arms and making everyone laugh.

"Can I help you?"

I turned and saw Zia, doughy fingers clasped in front of her.

"Hi," I said. "How are you?"

She pointed at me. "I recognize you."

"Yeah. I remember you."

Her expression went from warm to suspicious, as if she saw right through me. "You're here to eat?"

The jocularity of the booths went dead. Some signal must have been given, because I felt their eyes on me.

"No."

"Something else?"

Best to just get to it. "I'm looking for Antonio."

"He's not here."

"I..." What did I want to say? This was my last ditch effort, wasn't it? After this, I had nowhere else to look. "I mean him no harm. I'm here on my own."

She smiled. In that smile, I didn't see delight or kindness, but an emotion I'd inspired many times before. Pity.

I stood up straight. "I'm going to find him now or later, Zia. So, best now."

A man's voice came from behind me. "You want me to walk her out?"

I turned and saw the potbellied dominoes player. But I didn't move or offer to leave.

"It's woman stuff," Zia said, waving as if my appearance was just an inconvenience, not something heavy. She indicated the doors to the kitchen. "Come."

My phone vibrated in my pocket. I knew I needed to get back to the set. I would have to go in the kitchen, tell Antonio what I wanted and that I wasn't taking no for an answer, then hustle back. Zia walked me through the tiny commercial kitchen, past stock pots simmering on the stove and a man in a white baseball cap scrubbing a pan. I thought she was taking me to Antonio, but she opened a door to the parking lot.

"Zia," I said, "I don't understand."

"He's not here."

"Can I leave him a message?" I asked as I walked into the parking lot.

"If you think I'll deliver it."

"Why wouldn't you?"

She looked into the bright sun then back into the kitchen. "I have to go."

She tried to close the door, but I held it open. "Why?" I demanded. "Just tell me why. Is it a trust thing? You all think I'm running back to my ex with details?"

Zia took the doorknob so firmly that I knew I didn't have the strength to hold her back if she decided to close it for once and for all.

"Please," I said, taking my hand off the door, "I mean no harm. I swear."

"I believe you," she said. "What you mean, I know. But meaning harm and doing it? Not always the same."

"Is he okay?"

"Is he okay? *Si.* Until I kill him. Until I shake him out with my hands." She opened them and hooked her sausage fingers, shiny with years in the kitchen. "*Quel figlio di buona donna* asks me to cater a movie set. Doesn't tell me he's seducing you." She moved her hand up and down, tracing the vertical line of my body as if I was a monument to every girl he shouldn't be with. "*Stronzo.* That's what he is."

Her insults were affectionate, but she was very angry. I could pretend I didn't know what about me was so offensive, but I knew damn well it was my relationships, my culture, everything I was.

"Can you just tell him I was here?"

She shook her head as if I was an idiot. "No. If you chase him into our world, we will chase you out." She closed the door.

***

I thought of every worst-case scenario on the way to the set. Antonio was dead, in trouble, shipped back to Naples. He was responsible for the violence that had taken over the news channels, or he was the as-yet-undiscovered victim of it.

And I had nowhere else to look. I had no proof that anything was anything, and if I chased him, his world would chase me out.

On set that night, as I pondered the worst, I wasn't much more optimistic about Katrina. By the wide radius she kept around me, I could tell she sensed my discomfort. I kept my eyes on who was where, what buttons were unbuttoned, where arms and legs were placed, what lines dropped. It was the last day in the café. They were tearing it down. Nothing could be missed.

Then it broke like a fever. Katrina practically whispered "cut," and everyone cheered. It was over. We packed up for the umpteenth time, put everything back in the trucks. The affairs that had started during shooting would either amount to something or not. The friendships would be tested. If the movie would get to theaters depended on the next few weeks, and no one but me, Katrina, Michael, and the deepest Hollywood insiders knew how unlikely that was.

I got in the car, thinking I'd just take a midnight drive up Alameda and crawl into bed. I texted Antonio, even though it felt more and more like screaming down an empty alley.

*—I know I'm harassing you and I don't
care. If everything's okay just text
me anything back. A fuck you
would be sufficient—*

I waited ten minutes, watching the last of the PAs pack up. I was distracted by the silence of my phone. Tired of waiting for something that wasn't going to happen, I left.

Chapter 27.

Our final shoot had been in the West Valley, a straight shot down the 101. The freeway was relatively empty, and I went into auto pilot, listening to the news that the shootings and violence were unrelated, random. A southside gang shooting had hit the wrong man. A shooting during a robbery attempt. A beating in Griffith Park.

"The lady doth protest too much," I mumbled.

A Lexus cut me off as I was complaining to myself. I slammed the brakes, screeching and swerving as adrenaline dumped into my bloodstream. The Club slid out from under the passenger seat.

"Fuck!"

The Lexus picked up speed, and I did too. I was filled with a blinding hot anger. The Lexus swerved around, and I saw the man in driver seat. Young. Goatee. Flashing me his middle finger. He sped ahead, and I had no choice whatsoever.

I chased the car. I had no idea what I would do when I caught it, but I would catch it. It sped up even as it pulled off without a blinker. I rode his ass in my little blue car. Twenty-four, then twelve inches away at eighty. I was insane, not thinking like Theresa.

He didn't know who was in my car. I could have been a gangbanger, and he ran. Oh, if I caught him, what would I do... Choke. Kill. I couldn't imagine it any more than I could control it.

We landed on Mulholland, the most dangerous, twisted street to speed down, but we did. He would get an ass full of vintage BMW if he slammed to a stop, and I didn't know how to care. The Lexus turned so fast I almost missed it. We stopped on a private street with only our headlights illuminating the trees on either side of the road.

A bloated bag of unreleased rage, I grabbed the Club from the floor and got out of the car. "What the fuck is wrong with you?" I yelled from deep in my diaphragm.

His driver side door opened. I didn't have time to hope there was only one of them. I swung the Club at the nearest taillight. *Smash.*

That felt good. I went for the brake light.

"What the fuck?" shouted Goatee.

As the light smashed, I recognized him from Zia's. He'd been in a booth. I went at him with the Club, and he stepped back.

"Lady, you're fucking crazy."

He reached into his jacket just as the street flooded with light. Cars. I felt caught in the act and rescued at the same time. Goatee got his hand out of his jacket. He had a gun in it, but instead of shooting me, he shot at the cars pulling up behind me. A *ping* and a *clunk.* Another shot, and Goatee spun, screaming and clutching his bloody hand. His gun had been shot out of it.

Three car doors slammed behind me. I couldn't see the three men due to the backlighting, but I recognized the shape of a Maserati.

"Bruno, you dumb shit." It was Paulie.

When I felt strong hands on me, pulling on the Club, I knew it was Antonio. I felt like falling apart, but I didn't, even when I saw his dark eyes, their joy and charm gone. He had the face of a mafia capo.

I yanked the weapon away from Antonio and stepped forward, nailing the side of the Lexus on the foreswing. I aimed for Bruno's screaming head on the backswing. He ducked, and I swung again.

Everything happened at once. I was pulled back. Bruno's screaming stopped. Doors slammed. Road dirt sprayed my face.

Antonio shouted in Italian, and Paulie shouted back in English. A few *fucks* were the only words I understood.

I was in the passenger side of my car, and the car was moving. Fast. Antonio was driving. I held the Club up, and he grabbed it from me while driving with his other hand.

"You're fucking crazy, you know that?" he said.

He hit the gas, slipping the seat back to accommodate his height. In front of us, the Lexus took off, and Antonio chased it.

"Where were you?"

"Put your seatbelt on." He threw the Club into the back seat. "What did you think you were doing?"

"Breaking things!" Why was I screaming while I was obeying? "Not like it's your business, but I was going to crack his head open."

"Do you know who that was?"

Our car swung around a corner. Behind us, the Maserati followed, with Paulie at the wheel, I assumed.

"Bruno Uvoli," he said. "*Cazzo!* He's a made man. He'd sell his sister for a dollar. And you're like a fucking beacon, asking about me everywhere. What the fuck, Theresa? I'm trying to protect you, and you step in it. Deliberately."

"Answer a text next time."

We blasted into the Valley on the Lexus's tail, onto flat, wide boulevards and poorly lit side streets.

"Hold on." With one hand, he held me to the seat while he followed the car under a viaduct and out into a twisty service road, clipping the concrete wall in a shower of sparks. We were going seventy-five, and though I thought I should care about what my car would look like at the end of this, I didn't.

"I want you," I said, breathless. "I want you, and I'm going to have you. That's it."

"I'm death to you." He accelerated. The BMW kicked awake as if that was its shining moment.

"No. You're like mainlining life. I want it. I need it. I don't care what I have to do to earn your trust, I'll do it."

He pushed me down, swung the car right, then left, bumping the Lexus onto a turn up the foothills. The Maserati shot around us and in front of the Lexus, taking it in the side with a crunch.

"*Cazzo*," he growled again, but not to me. He screeched the BMW to a halt inches from the Lexus.

Paulie and Zo were already out of the Mas with their guns drawn.

Antonio unbuckled me with one hand and pulled my head onto his lap with the other. "Stay there."

I glanced up at him, his rock of an erection at my cheek.

He looked out the windshield. "I need you to drive away."

"You're not getting rid of me." I heard a scuffle outside.

"I don't want you seeing this. I don't want you near it."

"I'm not going back to Daniel with any of it."

"It doesn't matter. Look at you, ready to kill a man with a club. I've contaminated you enough." He slipped out from under me, opening the door and getting out.

I sat up. In my headlights, I saw how desolate the area Antonio had pushed the Lexus into was. Bruno was pinned to the ground by Paulie's foot on his busted hand. Zo knelt on him with one knee on his unbusted arm and the other on his thigh. Bruno's sneaker had been stuffed in his mouth to muffle his screams.

It all sunk in, what I'd gotten into and how. I froze, becoming myself again for a second.

Antonio leaned in the door. "Contessa. Drive."

"I want you."

"I heard you."

"You don't believe me." My eyes were locked on the pinned man.

"You want a man you imagine. If you knew who you were talking to, if you knew what I could turn you into, you'd run back to your DA." In my peripheral vision, I saw him take a pack of cigarettes from his pocket.

I turned to him. "Walk away. Don't do this. Not over a little road rage."

He lit the smoke with a clack of his silver lighter. "This wasn't road rage. He is stupid and dangerous. And he was after you. Now I have to make sure he never touches you, and that I never touch you." He closed the door and spoke through the open window. "Make no mistake, I will hurt you to protect you. Now go." He turned to the three men. "Zo, get off him, I got it. Drive her if she won't go."

"Yes, boss."

Antonio turned his back on me, and Zo approached. My beautiful capo didn't look back, only down at the man who had gotten me to chase him into a desolate area for a purpose I could only imagine, with the smoke and fire of hell winding around his fingertips.

Before Zo could reach me, I backed out and into the street. I didn't get far before I had to pull the car over. I covered my mouth with my hands and cried, muffling myself as tears fell down the cracks between my fingers.

What had I done?

Of all the things I could do from the front of my dented BMW, I had not one I *would* do. I could call 9-1-1. I could call Daniel. I could reveal the whole thing to the press. But I wouldn't, and I knew it.

And Antonio knew it. On some level, he trusted me.

Chapter 28.

I thought Katrina would come home and collapse, but when I walked in and found the house empty, I was the one who collapsed, throwing myself on the couch with my forearm over my eyes. They hurt from crying and would continue to hurt because the tears came again. I didn't even know what I was crying about exactly. Was it stress? Or the man I knew was going to die? Or the fact that I was responsible? Was it because I was pretty sure I had been about to kill him myself?

I don't know how long I laid there like that, but I fell asleep. I woke to a knock on the door. I looked out the peephole and felt so much relief that I whispered his name when I saw him. I opened the door.

"Contessa." His voice was rough.

"Capo." I leaned on the door, looking up at his eyes, sunken and tired and a little bloodshot. They flinched when I called him that then warmed.

"Send me away," he said. "Slam this door in my face."

I stepped aside and let him in.

"I tried to stay away," he said. "I've never wanted a woman this much in my life. I'd burn cities to have you. I'd fight armies. I'd commit murder to take you right now."

I grabbed his lapels and pulled off his jacket. He let me slide it down his arms. I didn't ask him any questions as I unbuttoned his cuffs. I didn't ask how he was when I undid the front of his shirt. I must have been a sight with my swollen eyes and stained cheeks.

He touched his thumb to the hollow of my eye. "You were crying."

I put my fingers on his lips, shushing him, and he kissed the tips.

"I can't keep away from you," he rasped.

"Don't. Don't ever." I took his hand. "Come. Let's wash tonight off."

I pulled him upstairs, walking backward. Halfway up, he lifted me. I hooked my legs around his waist and my arms around his shoulders, letting him carry me to my bedroom. We didn't kiss but kept our eyes open and our faces close, sharing breath and space.

He set me on my dresser. I finished unbuttoning his shirt and slid it off. I got his undershirt off so fast his gold charm clinked and dropped. That's when I noticed the yellow hospital wristband.

"What happened?" I asked.

"I'm fine."

"You were admitted."

"Somebody had to be. For the records. Otherwise they have to report a gunshot wound, even in the hand. Nobody wants that."

I inspected his face for a second.

"What is it, Contessa?"

"You took him to the hospital?"

"To a doctor I know at the hospital. We have people for emergencies."

My face got hot again. I felt my nose tingle and my eyes moisten. "You didn't kill him?"

"No."

A breath whooshed out of my mouth, and I cried with a smile. "I'm sorry. I'm so sorry. I just wanted to see you again. I didn't mean—" I was lost in tears.

"He's ambitious, and he saw an opening. What he did is past forgiving, but I kept seeing your face." He looked away and set his jaw. "If he comes near you again, I will kill him."

He held my chin in those powerful hands and tilted my face up. Our mouths crashed together. Our arms twined around each other, seeking purchase, finding it, and moving again.

He brought his lips to my ear and whispered, "When you left my office, I thought I'd never see you again, and it made me crazy. I was so angry at myself, I did stupid things it'll take years to fix. God forgive me."

I held him, kissing his neck and cheek with all the tenderness and forgiveness I could manage. It wasn't enough, not by a lot, but it was all I had. I wanted his skin against mine. I pulled my shirt off and twisted out of my bra.

Looking down, he touched my nipples with the backs of his fingers. "This is wrong. We're wrong. You and I. One of us is going to get the other one killed."

"I think about you all the time."

"I can't let you into my world. It won't work. They'll rip you to shreds."

"I touch myself thinking of you."

"I've done things I can never talk about. Even knowing what they are could hurt you."

I slid off the dresser and took his hands. "Come with me." I led him to the bathroom and turned on the shower. I wiggled out of my pants then reached for his waistband.

"This doesn't fix anything," he said.

"There's nothing to fix." I unfastened his trousers, and they dropped to the floor. I reached into his underwear and got out his cock. "This works."

"It's for fucking you."

I snapped the shower door open. "Never stop putting that cock in me."

He kissed me hard, pushing my head against the wall. "God help me. You make me crazy. We can't be together, but you're all I think about. Making you mine completely."

"I'll be yours. Let me be," I said.

"You'll be destroyed, Contessa. Peacetime is over. If anything happened to you—"

"We won't tell anyone. I'll be your secret, and you'll be mine. We'll meet in the night, when no one can see."

"It's too late for that."

"No, we'll say it's over. It's that, or nothing. If never seeing me again works for you, then go. I won't chase you again."

"Promise?" he asked.

His body relaxed, and I thought he was really going to go. It seemed impossible that his body wouldn't be pressed on mine, but it was his choice to make.

"I promise. I have the will to do it."

He put his nose to mine, his eyes scanning my face, then dropped his gaze. "I believe you." He kissed me, and the rigid pressure of his body returned. "You have the will, but I don't. I have to have you. Tonight and after, you're mine. Your first loyalty is to me. Every moan on your lips. Every wet drop from your cunt. When the thought of fucking crosses your mind, it's mine. Say it."

"I'm yours, Capo."

"No more halfway bullshit."

I swallowed nervously, because I didn't want to test our resolve or find out his desire truly was halfway, but I wanted to surrender completely to our pledge.

"I want your skin on my skin." I hated to bring it up, but it was my last chance. "After I found out Daniel cheated on me, I got tested for everything. I'm clean. And I left the IUD in."

He smiled, and my heart opened. "I'm a condom guy."

"Every time?"

"Of course."

"No halfway bullshit, then."

I got into the shower. He peeled off his underwear and joined me.

The water was hot and powerful. He leaned his head back and let it fall over his face in rivulets. The water darkened his lashes, making them stick together. I rolled the rectangle of soap in my hands then put them on his neck, running soap over the curves of his body. Shoulders, biceps, forearms, the space of his chest under the gold chain with the circle charm. He enfolded my hands in his, transferring the soap.

"What's this?" I asked, touching the gold medal.

"Saint Christopher. Patron saint of protection."

"Does it work?" I kissed it and the skin around it.

"Am I dead?"

I took his cock in my hand. "Apparently not."

Turning me, he put his hands between my shoulders, my ass, the backs of my thighs, then up the crack, massaging my pussy with his finger and my ass with his thumb. I picked up my leg and rested it on the ledge so he could get his fingers farther into me.

"Oh God, Antonio. I've wanted you for days."

"I'm going to fuck you so hard, little princess. I'm going to break you in two."

I twisted to face him. "Do it. Take me hard."

He looped his arm under my knee, pulling it up. The skin of his dick was so smooth on my pussy, he stretched and slid into me. He had to thrust twice more to get all the way in, hitching up my leg. He was so rough that I had no choice but to be a doll in his hands.

"You're so fucking hot," he said, pressing his thumb to my ass.

"Hard, please, Capo. Take me hard."

"Have you ever been fucked in the ass, little princess?"

"No."

"I'm taking your ass, right here." He grabbed my conditioner and squeezed the cold, viscous liquid down my crack. "Are you ready?"

"I don't know." I was nervous and admittedly aroused.

He fucked my pussy hard and wedged his fingers in my ass. "Your little ass is so tight. It's so sweet."

His fingers sliding in and out of me, stretching me, opened up new pleasure. "Oh, that feels so good."

He took his dick out of me and lodged it at my pucker. "You ready for me to fuck your ass?"

"Yes."

"Relax."

I tried to relax as he pushed forward. I had to brace against the tile, and he couldn't get in.

He reached around and put four fingers on my clit and his lips on the back of my neck. "Relax, sweet girl. Let me take you. Let me own you."

I groaned with the rising warmth under his fingers and relaxed. The head of his cock slid into me, and the invasion made me tense. I gasped.

"You are so fucking beautiful." He put his other arm tight around me and grabbed my breast. I felt bound and secure, unable to do anything but let go. "This ass was made for me."

He jammed forward, and I screamed, getting hot shower water in my mouth.

"What do you want, Contessa?"

He was asking if I was all right, and he waited for me to answer before he moved again. I needed a moment to breathe and took it. I shifted my hips until I felt better.

"I want you," I said. "I want you to fuck my virgin ass so hard."

He gripped me harder and pulled his dick out. The pleasure was overwhelming, reaching right to my clit, where his hand still gripped me.

"Take it," he growled in my ear as he slammed into me again.

"Oh, God. Fuck me in the ass."

"I love it. I love fucking your ass."

He pumped hard, rubbing my clit and stretching my ass farther than I thought possible. I kept whispering *take me take me* as the feeling of an impending explosion built. I went far away in my mind, past words, past thoughts, pain, pleasure. I was only his fingers and his cock, knowing me in a way I'd never been known before.

"You're going to come," he said. "I can feel it."

I grunted. The fuse sparked close to the keg, crackling and bright.

"Come on. Give it to me."

My ass clenched and pulsed around him, and my legs dropped under me. He held me up as I had the most powerful orgasm of my life, a slow motion detonation, every piece of flak airborne in its own sweet time, trailing smoke behind. I didn't realize I was screaming until the last bits of fiery shrapnel floated to the ground, as if I'd been unconscious. I woke to Antonio thrusting hard, slow, with a different rhythm.

"...in your ass, Contessa, *si, si, si...*" he whispered in Italian, sweet words I didn't understand.

"Come, Capo. Come inside me."

His groan was loud and final. A few more thrusts, and he molded his chest to my back, our rising and falling bodies matched in time.

"*Bene.*"

He kissed my shoulder. He pulled his dick from me, and I sucked in a breath.

"*Bene* is right," I said.

He stood up straight, and I turned around.

"Now we should shower, no?"

I laughed, and his smile lit up the room. We washed and toweled each other dry.

"Can you stay for a few hours?" I asked. "You can still slip out in the night."

"I have to take care of Uvoli, still. There are consequences to what happened with you and Bruno, and me. I have to talk with people." He reached for his clothes.

"I thought I saw him at Zia's."

"He's not my crew. He's a free agent. We keep him close. I'm saying nothing else."

I snapped his jacket away. It had his burned pine smell all over it. "Let me keep this then. To remember you when you're pretending you don't own me."

"While I'm telling lies about you?" He dropped his clothes and pulled the jacket from me.

"Tell me the lies. For practice."

He kissed my cheek. "I will tell them I fucked her once, and she got attached. But she knows the DA and will cause us trouble if she's hurt. I'll say I don't trust her. She means nothing to me."

"Like you said about Marina?"

"It was the truth about her." He pushed me onto the bed. "About you, I'll lie. Say you're not the most beautiful woman

I've met. You're not sexy. You're cold, unpleasant. Nothing a man would want to keep."

I touched his face, his lips, his stubble, his insane lashes. "What would it be like to be your girlfriend?"

He kissed my cheek and jaw. "We'd be friends first. And no touching."

"No touching?"

"No kissing, no touching."

"That wouldn't work."

He kissed my chest and breasts gently, little flicks of his tongue on my nipples. "You'd live with your parents, and I would come to visit you. We would sit and talk in the garden. Your mother would cook for me, and I would sit at the table with your family." He moved down to my belly, exploring every inch of it. "I would see you at church. Other men would talk to you, and I'd chase them away. Your father would hate me for a while. Then he would approve. I might touch your hand when no one is looking."

He got up on his knees and opened my legs. "I would fuck other women and you'd understand, because we hadn't even kissed." He brushed his lips inside my knee. "Then I'd ask your father for your hand, and when he said yes, I stop fucking other women." He ran his tongue inside my thigh. "You'd plan the wedding, and I'd work. I'd build myself. Being young and blind, I wouldn't see that you're now a target for my enemies."

He kissed my pussy gently. "You'd cry on our wedding night and call me a brute." His tongue flicked my clit. "You'd tell your mother I'm an animal. I'd promise to never fuck you like that again. I'd promise to be tender always." His tongue ran the length of my lips, circling the clit twice, then back to my opening. "It wouldn't matter. You'd be part of my life. My world. You'd get hard and cunning to survive, or you'd stay gentle and die."

"Antonio," I whispered, "can you do it like that? Can you do it gentle?"

He crawled up until we were face to face. *"Come vuoi tu."*

I pushed against him, feeling his hard cock on my pussy. My ass was sore, but I wanted him again already. He guided himself in, and I took him slowly, his shaft angled to rub against my clit.

"Oh, that's nice." I groaned.

He rocked against me, pushing all the way in. "You're so sexy. I love watching you walk, how your body moves under your clothes. How beautiful. How straight you are for the world, and how you bend and cry for me. I want to go so deep in you we have the same thoughts."

His eyes were unguarded, open, warm for me. The swelling in my pussy blossomed as I looked into his face. The sight and feeling mixed, becoming a swirl of emotion and sensation. We moved so slowly together that I felt everything, every inch of skin touching, every firing sliver of pleasure.

"I'm close, Contessa."

"Can you come with me?"

His face contorted with effort. "Soon. I'm trying to stay slow."

"You're amazing, Antonio. Amazing."

The last word barely made it out of my mouth as I was overcome with electricity. He jerked, slammed into me, and I cried out. He'd put me over the edge. I clawed his back as he jerked and thrust, growling my name. I spread my legs farther, feeling him against and inside me. We came as a crawling, rolling, single creature, as if we were having one orgasm. Even afterward, our breathing was the same and our hearts beat in time.

"I need to see you again soon," he said into my cheek.

"You'll come secretly in the night."

"Yes. I will. Be ready."

Downstairs, the door opened and banged shut.

"Maybe not so secretly," I said.

"Ah, this is the director?"

"Yeah."

"Is there another way out?"

"No," I said. "But I trust her."

He got up. "Good for you."

***

We went downstairs together, dressed and clean, to find Katrina standing in front of the television with a quart of salty vanilla ice cream and a spoon.

"You're up early," she called over her shoulder. "Did I wake... Oh, hello," she said when she turned. "Nice to see you again, Mister Spin."

"Katrina, you're up late. Or early, perhaps?"

She put her ice cream down and jammed the spoon into it. "Because I'm amazing!" She threw her arms up like a cheerleader.

"Oh dear, what now?" I crossed my arms.

"I got post-production financing!"

"Oh my god! How? Who? What?"

She said the next part so cheerfully, as if painting on a cartoon face. "Scott Mabat." She did a little jazz hands shake.

"What?" I yelled.

"*Gesu Christo!*" Antonio exclaimed.

Her knees bent, and her hands went from jazz to *stop*. "I have a plan."

"This better be good, Directrix."

"I take the money, start post, and get fresh financing from this German investor who's been sniffing around. I can keep the energy up, then just pay him off when the German money comes in."

"That guy"—Antonio pointed—"is a lowlife. Okay? He is worthless shit, and he's sick in the head. How much did you get from him?"

"Hundred thou," she said.

Antonio and I groaned.

"That's what it costs to finish a movie, guys. And that's cheap. I'm sorry but these are realities."

"Screw the Germans," I said. "I'm giving you the money."

"No, you're not."

"Yes, I am. I'll pay the note, and you'll be done with it." I turned to walk Antonio out. "Come on, I'll finish with her."

"Hey, Spin," called Katrina as I opened the door. "You should come to the wrap party Saturday night. Strong chance of epic."

"I'll think about it," he said.

I pushed him outside and closed the door behind us. The stars were drowned out by the light of Los Angeles.

"You're coming up with that kind of money?" he asked.

"Yes. My family is well-off. I have a trust, and I can use it for whatever I want."

He put his fingers on my chin. "I know all about your family. If Scott wants cash, you do not transport it by yourself. And you are not to see him without me. No negotiating."

"We're supposed to be a secret."

"Call him, don't see him. I'm serious. You don't know what you're exposing yourself to."

I put my hands on his chest. He'd left his jacket upstairs for me, and I felt his muscles through the shirt. "I'll stay away from all the loan sharks in Los Angeles."

"Please. I ask only this, please."

"How are you getting home? You came in my car."

"Don't worry about me."

I pulled away a little, so I could see the entirety of his face. "Don't feel pressured to answer this question."

"I won't."

"Did she stay gentle? Or did she become cunning and hard?"

"She stayed gentle."

I didn't feel right pressing him further. We kissed again, and I let him go.

Chapter 29.

A movie opening with Daniel seemed like the easiest, most convenient way to make sure Antonio and I didn't look attached. If he needed us to be a secret as long as possible, a few public sightings with Daniel Brower would do the trick.

—I'm going to a movie with Daniel—

He didn't return the text. I thought nothing of it. We were in stealth mode after all.

***

Big Girls was a huge, star-studded drama about a hot-button issue. The script was built for award-winning performances, and the director had a long career of pushing talent to the limit. So even without any car chases, explosions, aliens, terrorists, or trips to outer space, the film had been declared one for the historical lexicon.

I'd noticed the bald man outside the morning after Antonio left, and again when I'd gotten home from set. I saw him through the window, sometimes smoking or poking at his phone. I'd gotten close to him once, just long enough to confirm I didn't know him and the walking-through-dirt scent of Turkish cigarettes emanated from him. I didn't mention him to Gerry when

I confirmed I'd go to the movie with Daniel or when I met my ex outside the limo door.

I'd ended up agreeing to everything just for the sake of convenience. Even uptight, rich bitches had to deal with parking woes in Hollywood that were ameliorated with a limo.

"You look stunning."

"No flattery tonight, Dan. I'm just here to keep you from biting your nails."

He smiled and stopped me before I got in. "There are four guys in there. One is a bodyguard. The other three are going to talk my ear off about the press conference tomorrow."

"That's fine."

"I brought you this." He out held his hand. In his palm sat my engagement ring. I'd thrown it at him, huge stone and all.

Daniel had scrupulously saved to get me a ring that wouldn't embarrass him in front of my wealthy family. It hadn't mattered to me, but it mattered to him. He took me up to the Griffith Observatory on a night when Saturn was close and bright. He helped me onto the apple box as the astronomer showed me how to look into the telescope. There, with Saturn's rings as close and tangible as they'd ever be, he slipped the ring on my finger and said, "This ring around our world, Tink."

I picked up the ring. Did he say that? Or did he say, *my world?* Did it matter?

"You don't have to give it back," I said.

"The wronged party keeps the ring."

"No, the one who initiates the break up surrenders it. You would have stayed if I'd let you."

"Just take it." He opened the door. "One day, maybe you'll put it on again."

I got into the car, holding the ring. There were indeed four men in the back, and they did indeed talk strategy the whole way to the theater. Though I understood what they were talking about and I would have had plenty to contribute before the break up, I felt disconnected. It just wasn't fun anymore. I was watching animals in the zoo discuss their escape, but I was already outside. I'd moved on.

Cameras flashed, and Daniel answered questions as we entered. I smiled. I'd done it a hundred times, yet I couldn't believe I'd almost agreed to a life of it.

Right around the middle of the movie, the heroine and her husband had brutal, bruising sex, and I thought of Antonio. I wanted it again. Hard and fast with a side of hair pulling intensity, him grabbing me from behind as if he would tear me apart. When the movie ended and I stood, a drop of warm fluid escaped my underwear and ran down my thigh. I pressed my legs together to stop it.

"Are you okay?" Daniel asked as we got into the limo alone. The others seemed to have been dispensed with. "You seem flushed."

"I'm okay."

"I meant what I said." He touched my jaw by my ear, a move that had always made me shudder. "You are beautiful."

"What are you doing?"

"I'm seeing if I lost you," he whispered, coming close to me. I pushed him away. "No, Daniel. Just, no."

"I still love you. You know that."

I took a deep breath, and said something I never thought would be true. "I'm sorry Daniel. I don't love you anymore."

The mood in the back of the limo changed with an almost audible snap.

"It's him—"

"It's not."

"I can bring him up on murder charges tomorrow."

"I don't care."

"Fuck someone else," he pleaded. "Fall in love with anyone. Not him. All right? Just not him."

"It's over, I told you."

"He's a murderer." He looked as though he immediately regretted saying that. "I have no control around you. You leave, and I fall back into the guy I was because I can't be that guy around you. God, Tink, you were my valve."

"Daniel, I—"

"No, stop. Let me explain. I'm going to stick to the issue. This guy, I can't even say his name right now. That nice peacetime we've been enjoying? It's over as of last week. It started with a fistfight with one of his soldiers, and snowballed into what you've been seeing on the news."

Impassive. I couldn't let on, not even a little. What we intended to keep a secret in Antonio's world had to remain a secret in mine as well. Daniel wasn't above using his position to administrate his personal grudges.

"Daniel," I said firmly, "do not get distracted. You're trying to win an office in the second biggest city in the country."

"Not without you!" His voice got tight and sharp, his litigation voice. The voice of a man with a list of righteous grievances. "He killed Frankie Giraldi and Domenico Uvoli."

Uvoli. Bells rung, but I kept my face impassive.

"He came here for the men who raped his sister. Two, he tracked down and killed. The third, he's still looking for."

Nella. The sister he'd left behind.

"Do you want to know what he did to them?" Daniel asked.

"No." It felt ugly to be told like this. "Stop it."

"He castrated them, then he choked them with their own genitalia. In front of the men he needed to take over their businesses. What he did to find them, I can lay it out for you. You'll never say his name again."

"Stop it." I felt filthy hearing things I shouldn't from a man whose hurt was so apparent. "If you have proof, you need to prosecute. If you don't, you shouldn't gossip."

"It's not gossip when I'm talking to you—that's what I'm trying to say."

The car stopped at the building where Daniel and I used to live together. He looked at the front door, leaning over so he could see up to the eighth floor. Was he homesick? I didn't have the courage to ask.

He sat back. "When I failed you, you threw me out. I never blamed you, but I'm fighting for you. I'm going to win you back. Hell or high water, Tinkerbell. You'll be mine again."

Daniel opened the car for me and led me to the door, *his* door, without another word. I wondered if he could smell the Turkish cigarettes as he walked back to the limo looking more determined than ever.

***

The text came when I was almost asleep, from a number I didn't recognize.

—*Sweet dreams, Contessa. I will see you soon*—

I jumped at the phone.

—*Come now*—

My message bounced. The screen announced that number had been disconnected or was unavailable. I was relieved he'd sent me a text but disconcerted that the number was unavailable. What if I needed him?

I couldn't sleep. I put my hand under the sheets and slipped it beneath my underwear. I was soaked by just the thought of Antonio. My clit felt as sensitive as an open wound. I felt powerful, furious with desire, and I was going to come. My fingers wanted it as much as my engorged pussy. I counted to twenty, then I came forever, crying out for no one. When I was done, I cupped my pussy and looked at the ceiling, thanking God for the release.

My phone rang. Again, I didn't recognize the number. "Hello?"

Just breathing. A swallow.

"Antonio?"

No. It was a woman. On the off chance she was on a borrowed phone, I hedged my bets.

"Deirdre? Katrina?"

A sniff.

"Marina."

Still no answer. Just a weeping woman. What if she was me? What if Antonio was cheating on her? What if I was the mistress this time?

"Are you okay?" I asked. "There's no point calling if you're not going to tell me off or something."

"He's one of us," she croaked. "Not you. He's not one of you."

"I understand," I said, even though I didn't really.

"He thinks..." She choked a little before continuing. "I know him. He thinks you can make him something he's not."

"I don't know what he thinks, Marina. You should ask him."

She shot out a little laugh that must have soaked her phone in snot. "Maybe *you* should ask him."

I was about to answer, but she hung up.

Chapter 30.

Imagine being cooped up in small spaces with a hundred people in your age group, eight to eighteen hours a day, strictly focused on a project's completion. Imagine long waiting periods where you talk at length about the project and the most important thing in the world—the state of cinema. Imagine you connect intellectually and spiritually with those people. Imagine you can't connect physically because you're so busy.

Now imagine the party at the end of it.

"Honestly, I want to wait to hear from the Germans," Katrina yelled over the music.

It was the first time she'd been willing to entertain a serious discussion of my offer, and only then because she had a few drinks in her. Katrina and I had gotten a downtown loft that was between owners for the party. The rental and cleanup were paid for by the last pennies in the budget, and some sneaky dealing on my part paid for a DJ and open bar. People had melded into a simmering mass of hot, wet flesh pulsing with the music. The loft, someone's future overpriced home, had turned into a nightclub without the safety permits.

"If they fall though, I want a piece," I said. Meaning, a piece of the pie. I tried to couch it not as a charitable offering but an investment in something I believed in.

"You heard from crying lady again?" Katrina asked to change the subject.

"Nope." I hadn't heard from Antonio after his good night text, either. I didn't know what that meant. Did he plan to just come and go as he pleased? Were sweet little texts I couldn't respond to some kind of leash?

"Well, epic party ahead," Katrina said. "Maintain speed through intersections."

She grabbed my hand and dragged me into the middle of the loft where the thump of the music was the loudest and the press of bodies hottest. With the floor shaking, the kisses from the camera man, the bumping and grinding, and the gleeful exclamations over the music, I got diverted. Michael came up behind me, put his arm around my waist, and moved his hips with mine.

I let go. No Katrina and her money woes. No Antonio or his secrecy and lies. No Daniel, period. Just a fine-looking, nice man dancing behind me, a few more in front of me, smiles all around, and a feeling that I'd been part of something bigger than myself.

When Michael moved his arm, I kept dancing for a second. Then I felt a *whoosh* as an area behind me opened up. I turned with the music just in time to see Antonio throw Michael against a table. Michael bounced off the top and fell cleanly, like any actor worth his salt had been trained to do.

"Antonio!"

If he heard me over the music, he made no indication. He stepped forward, stiff and enraged. Michael, being the class clown, spread his legs, waggled his brows, and dodged. Antonio caught his wrist, the motion so fast and effortless that Michael was slammed against the wall with his arm twisted behind his back before I took three steps. A circle of stunned people surrounded the two men. Antonio was such a ball of power and rage that no one dared come near him.

"Maybe you shouldn't let her out by herself then," Michael grumbled when I got close enough to hear.

Antonio twisted his arm harder. I put my hands on Antonio's shoulders, tightening my fingers to make sure he felt them and knew it was me.

"Capo," I said in his ear, "he's my friend. Please."

Antonio's face was contorted in rage, and Michael was trying to smile rakishly through the pain. I pulled Antonio back, and he stepped against me. Michael turned and shook his arm out, giving his attacker a hot look.

"I'm sorry," I said, taking Antonio's hand.

"Put him on a leash," Michael said.

I feared Antonio'd take the bait and attack the actor again, but personal insults didn't seem cause for violence. He squeezed my hand and looked down at me, working his jaw.

"You have no right," I growled as the crowd dissipated.

"I have the only right. I'll hurt anyone who touches what's mine."

I knew we were being watched, so I smiled and touched his face. His jaw was tight and tense.

"Put a smile on your face or someone's going to call the cops," I said.

He stared at me with white hot intensity.

"I said smile."

He shut me up with a kiss. I must have tasted of sweat and hormones. The one beer I'd had was probably stale on my breath, but we kissed as if I was clean and fresh from the shower. Our tongues curled around each other, eating each other alive. His hands crept up my wet shirt, slipping under my bra.

"No," I said, turning away. "You can't just kiss me and make everything okay."

His mouth was on mine before I even finished. I pushed away with my arms, but my mouth had a mind of its own and stayed locked on his. My resolve melted like butter in a frying pan, leaving a streak of bubbling grease behind.

He put his hands on my face and moved an inch away. "You're mine. That means no pretty boys on the dance floor. No fake dates with the district attorney."

He must have seen me with Daniel on the news. Maybe in the paper. Maybe the man with the smelly Turkish cigarettes had told him.

"I'm not telling him anything about you," I said.

"I know you're not. In my heart, I know you have too much grace for treachery. But he wants to fuck you. I don't like it."

I wanted to draw the rules out for him in a cold, business-like manner. But I couldn't, and it wasn't just his beauty but the intensity of his gaze. Something spun inside him, some toxic lava. It terrified me, and it was the thing I wanted most. How could I draw lines around that? Was there a law I could lay down that it would obey?

"I can't see you with anyone else," he whispered into my ear. "It makes me crazy."

"We're supposed to be discreet. This isn't helping." He pushed his erection against me, and I gasped. "And where have you been? Your phone's disconnected."

"I've been busy."

"What the hell does that mean?"

"You're asking questions."

"I don't have the right to ask questions? Still?"

He held his finger up to my face. "I fuck you. I take care of you. That's what I offer."

"It's not enough."

"You American women make me crazy."

I closed my eyes for a second, getting a hold of myself. I couldn't fight him like this. He'd only come back at me like a bull.

"Tell me," I said. "Tell me what's happening. Where have you been? Are you all right?" I took him in, his eyes blacker, deeper from the moonlight coming through the window. "Don't tell me facts. Your truths all sound like lies anyway. I don't care about names and dates. I don't care about the situation. Just tell me about you. I want to know you, Capo." I touched his chest with the flat of my hand. "I want to know your heart."

"No, you don't."

"Let me know you."

"Contessa," he said so tenderly I barely heard it.

"Let me know you," I repeated. "Let me in."

He brushed a strand of hair off my cheek. "You dance with your friends. I don't. You see movies. I don't. You have a good life. I have something else."

"Come with me. You can dance too. We can go out to movies with friends, do all the things people do."

He put his arms around me and kissed me fully. When I slipped my hands under his jacket and felt the lump of a gun holster under his arm, he stiffened. I kissed him harder, because the feel of it had dumped a bucket of desire between my legs. I clutched him, the gun on the inside of my forearm.

He shook his head. "You turn me around every time. You're going to make me soft."

"A soft man wouldn't say that."

Something changed in his face. His jaw got tight again. "No, a soft man would." He grabbed my hand. "I'm taking you now, Contessa. And not gently."

We were in a room full of people. I had no idea what was on his mind, but he pulled me to the back of the loft and through the kitchen, which had been stripped to the lathe. He pushed through a metal door and yanked me into a fluorescent-drowned hallway with cracked walls and mottled concrete floor.

He rushed me into a dark closet and slammed the door behind him. Brooms and mops fell around us when he grabbed me, pulling my hair back and hitching up my skirt. The painted-over window let a little of the streetlights in, and when my eyes adjusted, I saw the fire in his eyes. Was this his reaction to a moment of softness?

"You're going to get me killed." He ran his fingers over my pussy roughly. "That make you wet?" He jerked my hair.

"Mercurial, much?"

"I will not die because you made me weak." He put me on the edge of the slop sink. I leaned on my hands, and he jerked my legs open.

"Fuck me then, you son of a bitch."

He ripped a gaping hole in my panties and shoved two fingers in me. With his other hand, he released his erection as if it was a weapon. He took his fingers out of me and put them on my throat, thumb and middle finger on each side of my jaw, pressing me to the windowsill.

"I fuck you, and you take it, do you understand?" Without waiting for an answer, he shoved his cock all the way in me in one thrust. The wind went out of me, and his hand on the throat kept me from speaking. He said, "You're mine. I am who I am, and I own you. That's all it is."

He fucked me hard and dirty. One hand pinned me by the throat, and the other hand spread my knee wide. My ass was balanced on the edge of a sink, and somehow, as rough as he was, his hands kept me from falling.

"You take it. Take it."

"Yes, yes," I croaked, pressure building every time his cock went in me.

He hooked his pussy-soaked fingers in my mouth. "Come, Contessa. Do what I tell you. Fucking come."

In three painful thrusts, I had to obey. I shuddered and cried out into his fingers, coming for him, only for him. He ground his teeth and plowed into me so hard, the pain was muffled by another rising orgasm. Still he came at me, punishing me with his dick, and still my body rose to him. He slowed, and I thought he was done, but he pounded twice more, lengthening my climax.

"Please stop." I gasped. "Please, Capo. I can't take it."

He sighed, shifted his hips, and gathered me in his arms. I wrapped my legs around him and rested my head on his shoulder.

"You're going to be my death," he said. "I don't know what to do. I feel weak around you. I'm going to slip up."

"I want to be there for you, but I can't. I can try to stay out of trouble," I said.

"I'm not worried about you getting into trouble. I'm worried about trouble coming to you. I'm worried about spreading myself too thin. I have enemies all around me. Every man wants his own thing, and not every man can have it."

I felt a light vibration at his hip. He ignored it and pulled his lips along my cheek, then to my ear.

"A bunch of my crew broke off. Is that enough for you to know?" he said.

"Yes."

"It's my fault, and it's going to take time to make right. I'll have someone on you."

"Will you come see me?"

"If I can."

His phone vibrated again. We kissed briefly before he dropped me, stepping back to button up his pants then his jacket. He checked me out and, finding me presentable, kissed my cheek and took my hand.

Back in the loft, in the middle of the crowd, he kissed my hand then stepped back. He bumped a girl in a tiny skirt then Michael. Michael held up his hands, and Antonio did the same before he spun on his heel and walked out, one hand on his phone.

Katrina crept up behind me. "Got a live wire on your hands, girl."

Michael passed by, a pretty girl on his arm, and said, "No dancing,"

I slapped his arm, but he walked to the dance floor with his new girl as if that sort of thing happened all the time.

Chapter 31.

Someone knocked at my door early the next morning. Katrina still wasn't home. I'd left the party twenty minutes after Antonio.

Looking out the window, I saw a bald man in jeans and a long black jacket. He was smoking. Would answering the door be stupid? Would that be getting myself into trouble? I decided not to risk it and let the curtain close. I waited one minute, then two, then looked out. He was gone, and a little package had been left behind.

I opened the door and peeked at the package without picking it up.

Contessa

Same handwriting as the cards on Antonio's flowers. I brought it inside and opened it. A phone dropped into my hand.

This device is secure. My number is on it. Please only use it for emergencies. And be very safe.

I checked and saw one number in the contacts with an area code in Nevada.

The front door opened, and I jumped. It was Katrina, and her lip was split.

"What happened?" I asked.

"He picked me up." Her breath hitched in a loud sob. "I got in the car, I didn't think anything of it. He said I lied about who I was. That I couldn't pay him back because no one was going to buy my movie."

"What did they do to you?" I said with an edge I didn't recognize from my own throat.

"The lip. It'll go away. I'll just make my vig until I prove him wrong"

I did something I'd only done once before, on the side of the road with a Club in my hand.

I lost my temper.

"What do you mean make your vig? Do you live in one of your goddamn movies? Who the hell even knew that fucking existed anymore?" I paced.

Katrina cried. She'd never seen me like that. *I'd* never seen me like that. I didn't even know who I was.

"I'm calling the cops!" My hand was shaking so hard, I couldn't dial before Katrina snapped the phone away.

"Central?" She spat the name of the LAPD's Downtown division like a curse. "Are you fucking with me? They're a bunch of blabbermouths. The editor of the *Calendar* has every one of them on the take. If this gets out, I'm finished."

"When what gets out? That he pulled you into a car and slapped you around? No. No. A thousand times *no*. I'll call Antonio."

"No! I don't want to be rescued by your boyfriend. That's weird. Forget it. Just forget it. I've handled douchebags like this before."

"How much do you need?"

She leaned on the back of the couch and pressed her fingers to her eyes. "A thousand for last week and a thousand for next."

"Interest compounded minutely if you don't pay." My arms were crossed. I was so mad, all my compassion had run away in fear.

"I can pay it all back when I get distribution. He just..." She drifted off, and tears welled again. "He didn't know about the lawsuit I lost. He found out. I think it just... I don't know."

"For someone so smart," I said, unable to stop myself, "you leave yourself open to the stupidest mistakes."

I stormed into my bedroom. My closet held a few thousand in small bills for emergencies. I counted out three grand and stuffed it in an envelope. I called Antonio from my new phone then hung up. Was this an emergency? Did he just tell me to stay away from Mabat because he was being protective? I really didn't want to bother him when he had so much going on. I'd apologize later for disobeying him if I had to.

I went downstairs. "Come on. I'm delivering it personally."

***

Katrina drove. The place was in East Hollywood, a trashy nightclub as big as my childhood living room. *Vtang.* I had no idea what it meant, but it was in big, flat red letters on the front, bathing the people in line in blood.

The bouncer, his hairline a receding M, moved the rope before we'd even slowed down. He ushered us past the register for the cover and into a room so dim I wouldn't have been able to tell the girls from boys if there had been no high hair involved.

I was still mad. I didn't know how I'd held onto it that long, because anger wasn't my forte. It was unattractive and uncontrollable. It pushed people away and for the most part, achieved nothing. This anger was mine, though, and it was a caged mink about to get skinned.

The bouncer nodded to the bartender and opened a door to the back room for us. We passed through then down steps, past a smaller door, into an underground office. I should have been scared, but I was too pissed off. Even when I saw four men lounging around the room, two playing backgammon, one on the phone, and one tending blood on his knuckles, I wasn't afraid.

Before anyone had a chance to explain our presence or introduce us, I spoke. "Which one of you is Scott Mabat?"

One middle-aged dirty-blond man in a black leather jacket, bent over the backgammon board, raised his hand slightly, the pointer extended to say, *one second.*

"Scotty, come on," the skinny guy across from him demanded. He pushed aside a tiny cup with a lemon peel in the saucer.

"Shut the fuck up, Vinny," Scott said.

"This is a fast-paced game."

Scott moved his piece. "Not when I play it." He stood. "Kat, nice to see you so soon. Who's the friend?"

"She's—"

"I'm the money." I wanted to throw the envelope down and storm out, but common sense cut through my anger. "I'm putting up her interest, and I'll be paying off her loan next week."

He stepped around the desk and slowly opened his top drawer. "Cash."

"Cash."

"I recognize your face." He flipped through a folder. "You marrying the district attorney?"

"No. Let's get this over with. I have last week, this week, and next week on me. I'll get you the—"

"Whoa, whoa, lady. Don't rush. Kat, did you explain that our terms changed?" He spoke to her as if she was a child.

I wanted to kill him slowly.

"No," she said.

I'd never seen her so cowed. She was the fucking Directrix, for Chrissakes.

"This is the contract," he said. "It's easy as shit. A moron could understand it. The studios give you a ream they nail together. You go to the Giraldis, they don't even write shit down. You're lucky." He flipped me two stapled pieces of paper. The contract was in bullet points and looked as if it had been the result of a hundred generations of photocopying.

"Point four," he said with his arms crossed. "Kat, would you like to read aloud to the class?"

She held out her hand for the pages. Was she insane? That docile girl couldn't direct a movie.

I read point four myself. "'Recipient has made no misrepresentation of their ability to repay the loan.'" I shrugged. "Okay, so?"

"So?" he said. "*So!*"

Throats cleared and chairs squeaked. A heightened intensity vibrated in the room.

Scott pointed his rigid finger at me as though he wanted to stab me. "This bitch didn't tell me she was *poison*. I put up half a mill on an Oscar nominee, not a whining cunt no one wants to touch. Her fucking shit's gonna be at the CineVention selling to Latvia for five G."

"A little underwriting would have gone a long way, Mister Mabat."

The guy whose knuckles were now fully bandaged snorted a laugh.

"That's fucking funny?" Scott said.

Knuckles shrugged. Scott, a man who could not be rushed through a game of backgammon, picked up a dirty coffee mug and bashed Knuckles in the back of the head so hard his neck seemed to shake back and forth like a seizure. It happened so fast, Knuckles's head had dropped to the table before either of the other guys could stand to aid him.

"This was easy money." Scott pointed the cup at me. There was blood and a single black hair on it. "A no-fucking-brainer. Terms changed. There are no prepayments. There's a thirty-year schedule she's keeping." He slapped the cup down. "We'll be happy to take it out of her ass when she can't shell out."

I was scared finally, but I didn't flinch. Knuckles was conscious and being tended by his two compatriots. Katrina sniffled behind me.

"Shush," I said to her. I held my chin up to the loan shark. "You will take the prepayment, plus five thousand, and you will be happy with that."

"Oh, really?"

"Really."

"Or what? You getting the mayor after me? I'm all grown now. He can't do shit."

I pressed my lips together in a smile. "He can't. But if you knew my name, you'd know I have a family. And if you knew anything about how they settle debts, you'd back away slowly." I pulled the envelope out of my jacket and plopped it on the desk.

"I suggest you do your research before dismissing my offer out of hand."

I dragged Katrina out by the forearm and didn't look back. I pulled her up the stairs, through the club, and into the street. I walked with my shoulders straight, confident that I owned everything in my sight. My friend blooped the car and got in. I followed and got into the passenger seat as if I was being chauffeured. It wasn't until Katrina stopped at a light on Temple that, in order to release the tension, I started crying.

Katrina rubbed my back. "Look, I'll pay what I can, and he'll get bored of me at some point. I mean, he can't make it so bad that I go to the cops." She laughed bitterly.

"Your memoir is going to be a blockbuster."

"*How To Ruin a Perfectly Good Career in Two Years.*"

"*The Girl With the Busted Kneecaps.*"

"Maybe I'll make him fall in love with me. I'll be Katrina Mabat."

"Oh God. No. You'd drive him to his ultimate death," I said.

"I think you should back off. Self-preservation is honorable."

"I'm paying him off and walking away. You'll release your movie, and everything will be back to normal."

She sighed and left the dead weight of it in the air. There was a shadow and a *clack clack clack* at the window that I recognized from my car breaking down in Mount Washington. Bald guy. Cigarette.

"Who's that?" Katrina asked.

"My shadow." I rolled down the window. "Hi. Can I help you?"

The smell of turned earth overwhelmed the air coming into the car. He handed me his phone. I hesitated.

"Spin," Turkish Cigarette Man said. "He wants to talk to you."

"Wow, Tee Dray. Wow, okay? Weird and possessive much?"

I took the phone. I had to stop myself from calling him *Capo* in front of Katrina.

He took the moment's pause to demand my attention in a tight voice. "Contessa?"

"Hi."

"You were in an Armenian nightclub? This somewhere you usually go?"

That was him asking me what I was doing without making assumptions. His tone was a coiled spring. He needed a flat truth, or he would wind himself tighter.

"I was seeing Scott Mabat."

He was silent, but in the background, I heard the mumblings of men, as if he was in a crowded room.

"Antonio?" I said.

"Otto will take you to me."

"No, I have—"

"He will pick you up and carry you." He would have been shouting if his voice had been raised, but he kept all the power and tension while practically whispering.

I knew then why he was capo. I hung up on him. I wouldn't disobey him, but I didn't have to tolerate the tone either.

"Kat," I said, "this guy's driving me to see Antonio. We're going to follow you home first and make sure you get in the door, okay?"

"Okay, Tee Dray." Her voice was suspicious even as her words were compliant.

I turned to Otto. "Okay?"

He held up his hands in surrender and smiled. Both of his pinkies were missing. "It's no problem." He had a thick accent.

He opened my car door. I started to get out, but Katrina put her hand on my forearm.

"Thank you," she said.

"It's no problem," I said in Otto's accent.

She smiled. "You're pretty badass. I didn't know that about you."

"Me neither."

Otto had parked his incredibly nondescript silver Corolla two spaces down, and he opened the back door for me.

When he got in, I said, "The car smells nice."

"*Grazie.* There's no smoking in the car. Still smells new, no?"

"It does."

"Okay, I take your friend home, then we go, okay?"

"Yes, sir."

***

"Where are we going?" I asked after we'd walked Katrina to the door.

Otto tapped on his phone from the front seat. "The office. But I confirm now."

"How long have you been watching me, Otto?"

He shrugged and pulled out. "A week. I sleep in the car. But no smoking in it. My wife, she's mad I'm not home, but I have a job to do until the boss tells me to stop doing it."

"I hope you get to see her again soon."

He waved the notion off with a flip of his four-fingered hand. "Spin, he save my life. She just make me crazy all the time. Watching you? Like a vacation."

"How did he save your life?"

"That is a long story, I promise."

"I have time."

He made a motion of locking his lips and throwing away the key. "Let him tell you. But he won't. He is too *modesto*."

"Antonio Spinelli? Modest?"

"Like a priest."

I bit back a laugh.

Chapter 32.

We approached East Side Motors. The yellow and black sign faded orange in the dimming light. The parking lot was clearer, so we pulled in without much trouble. Antonio stood in the middle of the lot in a black suit, waiting. The security lights cast a sunburst of shadows around him.

Otto pulled up. *"Buonasera,* boss."

"Thank you, Otto," Antonio said as he opened my door. "Go on inside and get coffee, then go home and rest."

"Grazie," Otto said and disappeared through the garage door.

Antonio took my hand, and I got out of the car.

"Contessa," Antonio said softly, his face deeply shadowed in the artificial light.

"Yes, Capo?"

He pushed me against the car. "I told you not to see him."

"He slapped Katrina around. I'm sorry, but I couldn't wait for you to take care of it."

"And did you take care of it?" His hands moved up my rib cage, thumbs tucking under my breasts.

I looked down. "Not really. He won't take prepayment. He made threats."

He held my face in one hand, a little too tight, to make me look him in the eye. "He threatened you?"

"He threatened Katrina." I pushed him off me. "I want to go home. My God, how did I let myself get stuck here?"

I pushed him hard, and he stepped back. Having gotten out from under him, I walked to the open gate. I didn't know where I was going. I guessed I'd have to call a cab. I could wait for it in the *pupuseria* down the street, but I knew he wouldn't let me go. I still wanted the freedom of that open gate and that dark street and those empty sidewalks. I heard him one step behind me, then he grabbed my forearm.

I twisted and yanked away. "Stop!"

His gaze was dark and unreadable for the second I saw him. He shifted, a blur in my vision, then he became a force of movement against me. He picked me up at the waist and carried me over his shoulder. I would have screamed, but he'd knocked the breath out of me. All I could do was watch the light shift on the blacktop as he carried me across it.

I pounded his back, but I was helpless. "Antonio!"

"Be quiet."

"Stop!"

"*Basta*, woman." He avoided the garage where Otto had gone and opened the door to the dark office without breaking his stride, passing the water cooler and the reception desk. He smacked open his office door then slammed it closed with his foot.

With a lung-emptying thud, I was dumped into a chair. He leaned over me, so threatening and powerful that if he demanded it, I'd have told him the sky was beneath my feet.

"Listen to me," he growled, putting his hands on the chair arms. "I will kill any bastard who touches you. So you walk into a room like that again without me, you'd better want the man dead."

He meant it. From the tightness in his lips and the lines in his brow, I knew he wasn't speaking metaphorically. He'd kill for me, and it would be my responsibility.

"I'll admit I was scared, and you were the first person I thought of," I said. "And the last person. But in between that, I was afraid of getting you involved."

"You're involved. I'm involved. We can't go backward now. You said you saw that stupid punk face to face, and I went crazy.

I saw you with that other ass, the one who cheated on you, and I went crazy. I don't have a brain when it comes to you. You know how much trouble it could be for me if I get arrested for something stupid? Like beating that guy with the ugly Porsche? But I thought he kicked you, and I lost my mind."

"You didn't even know me."

He continued as if I hadn't spoken. "When I was a young, they called me Tonio-botz because I'd go off over nothing. But I'm a man now, and I don't do that. Tonio-botz was a garbage kid who had no control over himself. But he's back every time I see you."

I was scared of him, for him, about him. I was also turned on. I touched his face. "I bet he wasn't so bad."

"Please understand."

"I do. Would you kiss me?"

With breakneck speed and intensity, he kissed me, using his tongue without prelude as if it was a dick shoved in me. I leaned up and he knelt back until we were both on the floor.

"Here." I pulled his wrist and slid his hand between my legs. "Feel how wet I am." I pressed his hand under my skirt to my damp panties, moving until his pinkie touched my soaking skin. "It's never been this easy, and it's you. This is how I react to you. It terrifies me."

He sucked air through his teeth. "We're even then, Contessa."

"Take me now, please. Fuck me scared."

He slipped two fingers in me all the way, pressing as if he wanted to get his whole hand in, and I spread my legs as if I wanted exactly the same thing. He put his face to mine until he took up the curves of my vision. His breath fell on my open mouth as he watched me react to his touch.

"I want to fuck you so hard we have the same skin."

"Yes," I gasped, reaching for his belt.

A knock came at the door. "Spin? You in there?"

"Fuck," he grumbled, then shouted to the door. "What, Zo?"

"Uh, sorry, but uh, we got word from Donna Maria. And you said—"

"All right." He removed his fingers from me.

Zo didn't get the message. "You said if we heard from her that—"

"Zo! *Basta*! I'll see you inside." He straightened my panties and skirt. "I'm sorry, Contessa. Business calls. You and I will share a skin later."

"Can Otto drive me home?"

"I'm sorry, but you're not going home tonight. I'll have one of the guys go to your house and pack you a bag. But until I take care of Scott Mabat, you're staying at my side." He stood, erection apparent under his pants.

I was still splayed on the floor. "Antonio, really?"

"Really. It's like the kids' shows. When the song comes, the bouncing ball tells you when to sing the words." He put his hand out to help me up. "Just follow along."

***

We crossed the parking lot holding hands, and when we went into the pitch dark garage, he squeezed my hand. I heard men talking and a *thup thup* sound.

"Follow along," he said and opened a door in the back.

In a low room decorated in wood paneling and cigarette smoke, a handful of men faced the same direction. Zo crooked his arm and straightened it quickly. A *thup* followed, and the others reacted by exchanging handslaps and cash.

Darts.

An Italian flag draped one wall. The chairs were wooden and well worn, like the desk and linoleum floor. I recognized a man in a fedora from outside Zia's restaurant. Silence fell on the room like a lead curtain.

Antonio kissed me on both cheeks, left first, then right. He stared me in the face for a second before facing his crew. "*Signori*, this is Theresa. Theresa, you've met Lorenzo."

Zo came up to me as if for the first time and took my hand. "*Piacere*." He kissed me on each cheek, right then left, and stepped back.

"Otto, you're still here?" Antonio said.

He stepped forward and took my hand. *"Piacere di conoscerla."* He kissed me the same way, left then right.

"Good to meet you," I said.

"Now go home," Antonio said. He indicated a man in a checked jacket and receding hairline. "Enzo, meet Theresa."

"Very nice to meet you," he said in a clean California accent I wouldn't have noticed in any other group.

"You, as well." I counted three more. Fedora was next.

"Niccolo, this is Theresa."

"Piacere." He kissed me quickly, in the middle of counting a stack of bills, as if the whole process was inconvenient.

"Nice to meet you, too."

"Last, Simone, I'd like you to meet Theresa."

"Good to meet you!" The only blond in the crew, he shook my hand like a car salesman and smiled big, only kissing each cheek when Antonio shot him a look. He did it right then left, and the mix-up meant we almost kissed on the lips. He laughed.

"Enzo, Niccolo," Antonio said, "go get the half-Armenian *strozzino*. Call me when you have him. Zo, bring the lady to the little house then pick her up a bag."

Otto, Enzo, and Niccolo left, chattering in deep voices.

"Antonio," I said with warning in my voice.

"The ball with the music," he said. "Please. Call your roommate and tell her Zo's coming."

"I have work tomorrow."

"I hope so." He whispered in my ear, "I'll come to you. Just wait."

Paulie burst in. "Hey! I heard there was a formal introduction."

"Hi, Paulie," I said.

"This is Theresa," Antonio said.

Paulie joyfully kissed my left cheek, then my right, and took me by the shoulders. "Welcome. Good to have you."

"Thanks," I said.

Paulie turned to Antonio. "We taking care of the Donna Maria thing?"

"Yes. Let me get Theresa set up, then we'll talk about it."

Chapter 33.

The little house stood up into the foothills behind a hundred feet of allergens. It could have been in the Tennessee mountains for all its foliage and acreage. A skinny kid of about nineteen with an acne problem sat on the porch. He stood when Zo and I drove up.

"Don," Zo said, "this is Theresa. The boss formally introduced her tonight."

"Huh," the kid huffed, as if surprised. "All right, then. *Piacere.*" His accent was terrible, but he kissed me on both cheeks, left then right.

"Donatello's gonna be on the porch. He's keeping his eyes on you so, don't worry about him." Zo punched the kid in the arm, and he almost fell over.

"Thanks," the kid said.

"This is a safe house, isn't it?" I said.

"Used to be. Now it's just safe."

He took me through the two-bedroom house, which looked more lived in than any safe house I'd seen in movies. I saw old world touches all over in the unfinished wood and hand-painted ceramics. The quilt on my bed was deep burgundy, the oil paintings showed seashores and mountains, and the kitchen, the only ultra-modern part of the house, had a basket of fresh fruit on the counter.

"This is Antonio's house?" I asked.

"Yeah."

"It's smaller than my loft."

Zo shrugged. "He likes it that way."

"Can you bring Katrina? It's her I'm worried about."

"Boss has it covered. He takes care of his people. And after tonight, you're with us." Zo kissed me on both cheeks again and left.

***

"Katrina? Are you all right?"

"I got a shard of swan in my foot, I want you to know."

I was curled up on a strange couch, in a strange house, with a strange guy on the porch to protect me. I had the news on and muted. The ticker moved, and the heads talked. "There's a guy coming to get a bag for me. Can you put some stuff in it?"

"Cups? Plates? Saucers? What do you want?"

"Are you okay?" I asked.

"When I'm not crying, I'm fine. God, I botched this."

"We'll make it right. I don't know how, but we will. It's a good movie."

"I'm going to my parents in the OC tomorrow. I'll stay a few days and get my shit together. If he chases me there, my dad will just shoot him."

"Great plan."

She sniffed. "Do you want the electric toothbrush? Or a regular one?"

"Regular. I don't intend to be gone long enough to charge the electric one."

"Okay. I gotta go. Michael's coming over."

"Really?"

Daniel's face appeared on the screen. The ticker told me he was doing the unprecedented: opening a major case against an organized crime family at the tail end of a mayoral campaign.

"Reckless asshole," I mumbled.

"Excuse me?"

"Nothing. Have fun with Michael. And, Kat?"

"Yes?"

"There are going to be men around watching you. Stay calm, okay?"

"Jesus, Tee Dray, what are you into?"

"I don't know, but I think I'm up to my eyeballs."

***

I slept on the couch until the navy sky faded into morning cyan. He came to me in a haze of pine and musk. His lips were my awakening, the hard firearm at his back a reflection of the hardness between his legs.

"Capo," I whispered through my sleep.

"Ah, Contessa. I could barely talk tonight. All I wanted to do was make peace so I could fuck you every day and night." He pulled up my shirt and kissed my belly.

"Is this about the trouble with your men?"

"Done for now. Tie up loose ends tomorrow." He pushed up my bra.

I wove my fingers in his hair when he sucked my nipples. "I can go to work?"

"Shh. No talking." He pulled away and got on his knees, looking at me. He yanked at my skirt and panties, slipping them off. "Spread your legs." He shrugged out of his jacket and pulled off his shirt. "Touch yourself." There was a sense of urgency about his manner as he wiggled out of the last of his clothes.

I watched him with my fingers between my legs, stroking my hardened, wet clit. "I want you so bad." I moaned. "I want you inside me."

"Shh." He put his cock at my opening. He thrust forward.

I put my hands on his shoulders, letting the thrust of his hips take me. He took my hands and pinned them to my sides, wrapping his arms around me tight. He pressed the whole of his body to mine as if he was trying to crawl into my skin. If he did, I couldn't have stopped him. He had me powerless under his weight, restrained by his desire. My legs were free but pinioned by the fulcrum of his cock.

"Every day," he whispered, "I'll take you like this. In the morning, before coffee, I fuck you. At night, I fuck you harder. In our bedroom, our living room, our kitchen, I'll love you in every room. *Mi amore,* I'll break you with my love and put you back together. And when I retire, you still call me Capo because you're mine. Always mine."

His lips spoke into my cheek. I felt wrapped in him, past, present and future. I had no whim or hunger outside the building pleasure in my legs and safe pressure of his skin and muscle.

I gasped. I was going to come. I wondered if my explosion would be held down, tamped by the weight of his arms and the swirling affection in his words. But my orgasm came in a flood. My back arched, and my thighs got stiff. I saw nothing, heard nothing, felt nothing but Antonio. His weight, his breath, his scent, and his pleasure, concurrent with mine, swirled together inside my skin, and I, inside his.

***

We stayed wrapped around each other for a long time, just breathing together. I was so tired, I fell asleep under him. He whispered *mi amore,* kissing my neck and shoulders, then relaxed his arms.

"My Capo," I said. "Always."

"You should sleep." He brushed wet strands of hair from my face as if it was of great concern. "I brought your bag."

"I hope she packed work clothes."

"You stay here today. I haven't taken care of the *strozzino* yet."

"Antonio, please. I have to live."

He pressed his fingers to my lips. "What do you think happened last night?"

"I followed the bouncing ball."

"You are under my protection. My crew recognizes you. They can't touch you, and they will protect you. But you also have a responsibility to us to stay out of trouble. For a few days, things will be disrupted. Bruno and Vito, they're doing their own thing. I didn't want that. Vito, with the young girls..." He rubbed his eyes. "I don't like it, but…" He looked up and crooked his neck as if shaking off the thought. "We have to pay tribute to another family, so everyone recognizes them as their own thing, not just us. This has to be completed before I can let you walk around without an escort."

"What?" I sat up, and he moved off me.

"I couldn't isolate you and keep you safe. This was the only way. You're untouchable now, as long as you obey the rules."

"What are the rules?"

"Do not talk to the press or police. Not talk about our business with anyone. Not ask questions." He held up his hand to my pending objections. "You can ask *me*. But no one else. I have all the information. My men only know some things, and if they talk, you get half the story. And I know what can hurt you."

"You might have mentioned this before all the double kissing happened."

"What am I asking? That you be loyal? That you come to me first? Only the saying of it makes you sit up and cross your arms."

I huffed. Of course he was right. Of course I had no intention of ratting him out or investigating him further. It was indeed the list of rules that bristled me.

"This needs to be on a probationary basis," I said.

"One minute probation," he said then kissed me, his hand tight on my jaw, his tongue prying my mouth open. He stopped. "My minute's up, Contessa. Are you still mine?"

"You are my Capo," I whispered. "But I'm mad at you."

"Get in the shower then before I fuck you again."

***

Katrina had packed everything I needed. One set of work clothes, one set of regular clothes. Shoes, toiletries, and a note.

Tee - Thank you for everything. You are a shining star. I promise not to let you down. You'll be proud of me one day.

Be safe, okay?

The Directrix

When I got out of the bathroom, Antonio held up my phone. "What are we going to do about this guy?"

There was a text from Daniel.

—need to speak with you in person by tomorrow—

"What are we going to do about you looking at my texts?"

"As long as you're talking to him and the thing is face up on the table, I'll look."

"You don't trust me?" I asked.

"I do."

"I think you're missing an opportunity to get some inside information, Capo."

He crossed his arms and narrowed his gaze. "Contessa."

"If I don't see him, he's going to get suspicious. He's just opened a case against, I'm assuming, you? Knowing I might be with you? Let me see him and find out what he wants."

"You're going to spy for me? I don't want that from you, ever."

"To be honest, I just want to go home and have kind of a normal day. You know, one where I don't see a gun or take part in some ritual I don't understand."

"And you need to see Daniel Brower to do that?"

"He's not a loan shark or a baby capo looking for territory. He's not going to hate you any more than he already does, and he'll never touch me. What's the harm in me putting on my work clothes and taking a lunch?" I put my hands on his forearms, and he dropped them. "We'll be in public. I promise." I slipped my hands around his waist and held him close.

He put his arms around me and kissed my head. "*Come vuoi tu.*"

Chapter 34

Enzo drove me home in a charcoal grey Ferrari and left me in the parking lot. I went right to my car and made it to work just in time.

Pam was business as usual, dozen red roses on her desk notwithstanding.

"Good morning," I said.

"Morning."

"What do I have today?"

Pam rattled off a list of meeting and conferences. I texted Daniel.

—What time today?—

—Stuff exploded. Tomorrow ok?
Before lunch, 30 min?—

—No prob—

"Can you reserve the big conference room at eleven thirty tomorrow?" I asked Pam.

She tapped around. "It's free. Who are you meeting?"

I looked over her shoulder. The blinking cursor required an answer to who would be in the room with me. "Daniel Brower."

She tapped it in, her expression sour under her rhinestone-tipped horn rims. "You know, polling this morning shows he's in the lead for mayor."

I plucked the card from the roses. "I knew he didn't need me to win."

Tonight.

I smiled to myself. Tonight, indeed.

***

I tried to keep my mind on my meetings and rows of numbers. I smoothed things over between two accountants on my team while thinking about Antonio's body. I didn't know how much longer I could stay at WDE. I hadn't been fully engaged in my job in months. After spending time with Antonio, the job felt like a blunter, dimmer version of life.

I kept Antonio's phone in my pocket. When it rang during a meeting, I excused myself and answered in the hall. "Capo?"

"Paulie."

I might have blushed, as if he'd walked in on my dirty thoughts. "Hi, Paulie."

"I'm coming to pick you up from work. Is six okay?"

"Sure. I can leave my car in the lot."

"See you then."

***

Our valet was in the alley behind the building, and Paulie's Ferrari fit right in. When I came out, he was leaning against it in the shade of a bougainvillea hedge, smoking a cigarette.

"Hey," I said. "What happened to you?" I pointed to my lower lip, indicating the split on the bottom of his.

"Fell on a guy's fist."

"You should watch where you're walking."

"He's taken care of. You can tell your friend the loan's forgiven."

"I'll give him his money. I don't want to steal it," I said.

"Don't worry about it."

He opened the passenger door, and I got in. He obviously didn't want to discuss the money. I'd wait, but I had every intention of making sure Katrina's production was clean.

"Where are we going?" I asked.

"San Pedro."

"We going to the beach?" I asked facetiously. San Pedro did indeed have a beach. It was also home to the loading docks and a notorious organized crime stronghold.

"We have an office down there."

"Of course you do."

With that, he drove into the traffic of Wilshire Boulevard.

"Where are you from, Paulie? You sound American."

"Here. Born and raised. Pure-blooded Angelino dego."

"Have you always been, um, in the life?"

He flung his hand back, as if indicating everything behind him. "Few generations. I'm as in it as Spin."

"And you guys partnered? I mean, were you here first? Did he just muscle in or what?"

"He told me you were full of questions."

"Did he tell you how frustrating it is to not ask any?"

He swung south onto LaCienega. "Doesn't occur to me. I stay inside the lines. Safer that way. No questions because everyone already knows the answers."

I didn't say anything all the way down to the 10 freeway. He went east, and the wind drowned us out.

Paulie started talking as if he'd been working on his answer the whole time. "Spin came here with a bloodline, which is important. Gives him credibility, you know? He came right to me and asked for my permission to do some business. Did it exactly right, too."

"I can't imagine him asking permission to do anything."

"Wasn't like I couldn't tell right away he could run a crew. And I'll tell you, it would have been stupid for me not to partner up."

"Why?"

"Because I like money, that's why," he said.

"He knows how to get it, I presume?"

When he didn't answer, I thought I'd said too much, pushed him past his comfort level. He rubbed his lip as he changed lanes.

"How did your family get their money?" he asked.

"Generations of stealing followed by a few generations of legalized thievery. Now it's all compounded interest."

He laughed. "You're honest."

"Sometimes."

"I'm going to be honest with you then."

"Oh, this is already so much better than that meeting I cancelled."

"My partner, he likes you."

I was going to joke about being relieved but decided against it. This seemed very serious to him, so I shut up.

"He introduced you. That doesn't happen every day. He's got girls who are in the life. Like family." He turned to me briefly then looked back at the road. "Do you know what I mean by that?"

"I think so."

"Okay, so none of them are anything. But you? He's lost his shit. He's pissing himself. After today, shit's gonna change, and I don't know if you can handle it."

"Are you sure he'd want you telling me this?"

"I'm not telling you anything you can use. Reason is, and I'm being honest here, I don't trust you."

I watched the train stops in the center of the 110. The road was relatively clear. Paulie kept left, and everyone got out of the way.

"I guess I don't blame you," I said.

The paper bag-brown sky of San Pedro crept over the horizon. Giant chair-shaped cranes loomed over the portal to the sea.

"Thanks for helping with my sister that night," I said.

"No problem."

"You were very level-headed."

"Thanks. You too."

Chapter 35.

Paulie pulled into the docking area with a wave. Yellow and black striped barriers went up everywhere, allowing a right, then a left, to an alcove inside a parking lot that housed two trailers and a couple of cars.

"You really know how to schmooze a girl, Paulie."

He winked at me, and we got out. I followed him to two red shipping containers fifty feet from a sheer concrete drop to the fouled water of the harbor.

"Okay, kid, here's the deal," Paulie said. "You're not going to care for this, but you're going in there with me. I am not going to hurt you. I'm not going to hurt anyone you care about. I'm telling the truth when I say you need to see something."

I hadn't been nervous. I knew Antonio was at the end of this journey, so I'd felt safe. As Paulie spoke, I became unsure and my heart pounded. The container had no windows or doors. Once I went in, I could be easily trapped.

"Let's go then," I said.

He grabbed the silver pole and yanked it down with a clack. He swung the door open, and it creaked so loudly I was reminded of a horror movie. When the triangle of light cut the dark tunnel, I had second thoughts.

"I'll leave the door open a crack," Paulie said.

"You coming in with me?"

"Right behind you."

I didn't feel safe. I didn't feel threatened, but I didn't delude myself into thinking Paulie would jump a pack of wolves for me, double kiss or not. I stepped up to the entrance anyway. Maybe curiosity drove me. Maybe a quest for self-destruction. Maybe I wanted to grab a little badass cred and put it in my Prada bag or walk in riskier shoes.

Two steps in, I heard wet, arrhythmic breathing. Then the door closed, and the box went dark.

"You said you were leaving the door open," I said.

"Oops."

The light flicked on, drowning the tunnel in flat, industrial illumination. A man was curled against the wall, his ankle chained to a hook on the side of the container. I'd thought I was nervous and scared before. But when the door opened again, I understood what it felt like to jump out of my own skin.

Paulie laughed. He leaned on the wall casually tapping his phone.

Zo stuck his head in. "There you are."

"Come on in," Paulie said.

"Hi, Miss Drazen," Zo said. "How you doing?"

"I'm fine."

Zo glanced at Paulie then the guy.

"She's cool," Paulie said. "Let's see him."

Snapping the door shut, Zo crossed the length of the shipping container in about four steps. He kicked the guy to semi-consciousness. "Hey, asshole."

He picked up the man by the back of his collar. His face was beaten bloody, but I still recognized Scott Mabat. Zo plucked a bottle of soda from his jacket pocket and shook it before tossing it to Paulie. Paulie nodded as he passed me, tapping the bottle cap to his forehead as if tipping his cap to me. It left a dot of condensation. The soda must be ice cold.

"Time to get up, Scotty." Paulie opened the bottle into Mabat's face.

"Fuck!" Scott yelped.

"Welcome back."

"Fuck you!" He spat blood.

"I know it's been a rough night. So I brought you something pretty to look at." Paulie yanked Scott's face around until I was in his line of sight.

Shit. I had to decide what to do quickly, and I decided to do what I always did. Show nothing. Give nothing. Own it.

"Where's Antonio?" I asked.

"Taking care of business. He's on his way."

"Fucking frigid bitch," Scott said.

"Same wonderful sense of humor, I see." I said.

Zo laughed long and loud then petered.

Paulie capped the soda bottle and turned to me. "So I have a problem, and I think you can help me solve it. Scotty here is the victim of my partner's protective streak. I didn't know he had one. But it's there."

Scott coughed and sputtered. "I'm gonna fucking kill you." He stared at me then coughed again.

"You're being paid, Mister Mabat. I have the money ready to be wired." I clipped every word, keeping it business despite the piss I smelled on him. I refused to be sick. I refused to even have a feeling about what was happening. Now wasn't the time for feelings, only thoughts. Cold ones. I couldn't get muddied.

"Fuck the money," Scott said. "I'm getting your friend's tits."

"See," Paulie continued, before I could snap back at Scott. "I have this trust thing with you, like we talked about. So I looked into you, your whole family. You're clean, but a couple of you got your fingers in shady pies. Your father could teach me something about the business."

"And you could teach Scott something about the importance of research."

Paulie's mouth tightened, and I knew he was holding back a smile. "You hear that, Scotty? You taking notes?"

"I'm gonna put my fist up her little Viet-cong ass," Scott growled at me.

"Yeah," Paulie said. "Scotty over here is touching on something I'm getting to."

"Make her suck my fingers after."

"Shut up, douche." Zo slapped Scott, sending a splash of blood to the wall.

I noticed then that there was no blood on the walls or floor. A gruesome observation, but it told me that he'd been beaten and moved there.

"Personally," Paulie continued, "I like you. I think I mighta fucked you if Spin wasn't already whipped. But here you are, hanging around the neighborhood, DA's girlfriend, looking for shit. So I'm nervous. Then there you are, being introduced, and I can't say shit. Even if it's common sense, I gotta button it because those are the rules. Everyone's got rules but the women."

"I got pulled in. You forget."

"No. I didn't forget, and I don't care what you do on purpose," Paulie said. "This whole thing with Vito? Spin was already pissed he had a valet thing on the side. A straight job, no less. But then he beat his ass over some bullshit about a girl he didn't even know. And why? Because he's pussy whipped. Then Bruno partners up with Vito, and I got two guys Spin's after, guns blazing. He's beating on their friends trying to find them. Four days, my partner didn't make no sense. Four days he forgot the rules, and everyone runs to Donna Maria looking for help. It gets so bad he's gotta ask permission from another family to do what's his right to do. Now I'm dragged in, thinking you must have a magic cunt."

Scott scooted around on his knees. His hands were tied behind his back, and one shoulder looked dislocated. He needed a hospital stay.

"Here's what I told our boy here," Paulie continued. "I told him I'm not gonna kill him. I told him you were an accessory to all this. And I told him he couldn't touch you. You are protected, by us, indefinitely. This will keep my partner happy, and you alive, because this guy's pissed." He pushed Scott down with his foot. "Right, you Armenian fuck? You're pissed, right?"

Scott tried to spit on him, but gravity put the spit back on his face. Paulie leaned closer, in spit range, but Scott didn't appear to have a drop of saliva left.

"You're gonna take it out on someone, aren't you?" Paulie asked.

Scott smiled through a bloody mouth.

"You sold him Katrina," I whispered.

"Maybe. That's up to you."

He stepped back and let Scott and me look at each other. Worry and fear crept through my skin. Resist them though I might, I wasn't calloused to this. I was a nice girl with a beach house and perfect grades.

"Well then, Mister Patalano, it looks like I'm going to have to figure something out." I turned to leave, but Paulie held me back with a hand to my shoulder.

"I'm not done."

"I disagree."

"You can run to the DA. You can run to daddy. But I know your father better than you do, even if I never met him. Our families aren't strangers, if you know what I mean. And the DA? Don't get me started. Your girlfriend has a couple of family here in Orange County. A few friends. She disappears, it's in the news this week, and next week London Westin's worn-out pussy's in the papers."

He reached in his jacket. He was going for his gun. I think my panic must have been visible then, because he held out his hand to calm me. He slowly pulled the firearm.

"I have a solution for you," Paulie said. "You want to earn my trust? If you earn that, you and your girlfriend will be under my protection. This guy won't touch either of you." He handed me the gun.

Zo spoke up, "Paulie, whoa! The fuck?"

"Shut up, Zo." It sat in the flat of his hand like an offering. "Take him out. Problem solved."

Scott laughed, lightly at first. Maybe a smarter person than I am would have deduced another solution. Maybe a more naturally manipulative person would have stalled long enough to change the course of events. But I was empty. I took the gun. It was lighter than I expected. Easier to pick up. Maybe I thought it should weigh some more supernatural amount, equal to the death inside it.

"Take him out, and you're going to solve all kinds of problems," Paulie said.

"You're nuts, you know that?"

"I'm hedging a bet. It's a million to one you have the spine for it. And I gotta be honest, I want you out of the picture."

"Paulie, come on," Zo said.

"Shut the fuck up, Zo." The man with the bow lips stood close to me, engaging in a staring contest I had no intention of losing.

"She can't get made, no ways," Zo pleaded.

I said softly, "This is a very risky proposition."

"No, it's not."

"Shit." Zo was freaking out. "Pauls, what if she misses and hits me?"

"Pick him up," Paulie said without releasing me from his gaze. "Let her get a good shot."

"I'm not killing anyone," I said.

"My money's on you not even pulling the trigger."

"Does Antonio know about this little bet with yourself?"

As if in answer, Paulie's phone buzzed. He ignored it. "He's not here right now, is he? He's busy taking out two perfectly good guys he alienated because of you. I'm here cleaning up this mess he made because of who? Yeah. You."

Scott had stopped laughing, the blood on his lips crusting over. Paulie squeezed my hand with the gun in it. He looked at it, and I followed his gaze. The gun was hard and black with flat surfaces and squared edges. A cop gun, not a cowboy gun.

I slipped my finger in the metal loop around the trigger, cupping the handle in my palm. "You misread me, Mister Patalano. You think I'm some sheltered little girl who never had to fight for myself. But I've spent my whole life fighting for myself. Just not the way you think."

"Prove it." His phone buzzed again.

Was it Antonio? Could I stall long enough to get a bye in this little game?

"She can't earn no bones anyway, Paulie, come on!" Zo was near hysteria.

"Aw, the little girl has a gun?" Scotty said.

I didn't know what was wrong with him, why he didn't just roll over or shut up. I didn't know what had to happen to make him continue taunting his attackers until they killed him, but whatever it was, Scott Mabat was in self-destruct mode.

So I pointed the gun at him. "I could shoot you right now."

"You don't have the balls. My dogs will rip that girl in the middle."

He didn't threaten me. He'd never threatened me, only Kat. As if he thought that in self-preservation, I'd just let her get pulled into a basement by him and his cronies. And he'd leave me unharmed at the door. Paulie's word must really mean something.

"I'm going to shoot you, Mister Mabat, unless you allow a prepayment and keep your hands off Katrina," I said.

"You're not shooting anyone."

"Keep making me angry."

"I bet she tastes like soy sauce when she cries."

My hand tightened to the point of no return. I pulled the trigger. Tight. Tighter, until the tension in the thing released, and the trigger bounced back.

Nothing happened.

Scott broke into hysteria.

Zo's eyes went wide. He chanted "Holy shit holy mother of Jesus," over and over.

I let the gun swing from the trigger loop, finger extended. Paulie looked both impressed and pensive as he held out his hand for it. We didn't have a chance to exchange a word because the door opened with a creak.

Antonio stood in the rectangle of light. "Paulie." The word was a statement with a serious undercurrent of darkness, violence, and unspoken threats. "What is she doing here?"

"Nice to see you, too. What took you so long?"

Antonio stepped inside, taking in everything, his hands, knuckles already bloodied and bruised, coiled for something. Zo shut up as if someone had stapled his mouth shut, and Scott, for once, was reduced to silence.

"You said you were in the trailer," he said.

"I moved him."

Antonio reached me and took the gun then put his other hand in mine. I realized that with everything we'd done together, we'd never held hands. Not until I was afraid to hurt him or get blood on my cuffs did I feel his fingers laced in mine.

"What the fuck are you doing, Paulie?" Antonio asked.

"Good luck with this one," he said.

Antonio pulled me through the door, and I followed because I had no choice. Though the container had been lit, the afternoon sunlight made me squint. I held my hand up to block the sun as Antonio pulled me toward his Mas.

He opened the door for me. "Get in, and do not make me put you in."

I got in. He came around the front of the car. We watched the open door of the red shipping container. No one came out. Antonio backed out of the parking lot in a spray of gravel.

"What the fuck—"

"He picked me up from work," I said.

"What did he tell you?"

"Nothing. Then we went in there, and Scott looked like that. Did you do that to him?"

"I didn't want you to see that. It was supposed to be that I finished getting his guys to understand my position, then we worked on Scott. Then you gave him his money back, and you were done."

"Well, I did see it. You hurt him. One of his eyes was sealed shut."

"I woulda done worse if Zo hadn't pulled me off him." Antonio drove in a rage, pulling onto the freeway as if he wanted the car to eat it. "He just wouldn't stop fucking talking. This is what I was telling you. This is who I am. This is what you do to me. And Paulie? He doesn't trust you. He showed you so you'd run away from me, right?"

"He wanted me to shoot Mabat in exchange for Katrina's immunity."

"And what happened when you wouldn't?" he asked.

"I did."

"You what?"

"I pulled the trigger."

I saw that he was confused. He was probably thinking: Had Scott been quiet when he got there? Did he look dead? Who was the woman sitting next to him? Was there a whole new set of problems to solve?

"You think you're the only one, Antonio. You think you're the only one with a little murder in him," I said. "A little temper? Well, I knew there were no bullets in the gun, because it was so light. I knew it would just click, but I was sorry it was empty. I wanted to spray his brains all over the wall. He's a waste of a man."

Antonio pulled the wheel hard right at eighty miles an hour and screeched to a stop at the shoulder. If that was what it was to be mercurial and impulsive, I understood the appeal. Every moment felt like living at the height of awareness, every sense sharpened to a fine edge.

"God help me," he said. "I've ruined you."

I touched his arm, but he pulled away.

Chapter 36.

"Antonio," I said.

He didn't answer, just kept his wrist on the top of the steering wheel.

"Capo."

"Don't call me that."

My face got hot, and my loins tingled as if I'd been dropped off the first hill of a roller coaster. I wanted to look at him, but I couldn't. I wanted to check his hands for bruises and accuse him of worse violence than I'd wanted to commit. I wanted to make excuses and demands. I looked at my own hands, free of blood or bruise, but they were shaking.

"Antonio, what's wrong?"

He got off the freeway downtown. "It doesn't matter."

"I think it does."

"We'll still protect you."

"What? Wait. I don't understand. What happened to everything?"

"It's just done, Theresa. Over." He shook his head, eyes on the road and avoiding my gaze.

I blinked, and a tear fell. What had I done? How could I have done differently? How could he shut me out? "This was Paulie's plan? That you'd hate me?"

He didn't answer. He'd turned to stone right in front of me.

"Brilliant," I muttered. "He's a fucking genius."

"Nice mouth."

"Fuck, fuck, fuck!" I hit him on the arm.

He yanked the car over, screeching to the curb a few blocks from the loft. He drew his finger like a rod, rigid and forceful, as if he could kill me with it. "Do not hit me again."

"What happened?"

"This is not what I want. I'm in the life. I'm damned, I know this. I cannot come home to a woman I'll share hell with." He slapped the car in park and turned away from me again, as if seeking answers in the half distance.

"You would have done the same to protect someone you cared about," I said.

"I would have beaten him to death with the empty gun. That's the point, isn't it?"

"I'm not understanding the point."

"Please just go. I don't want to see you again."

His words tightened in my gut, twisting my insides to jelly. "Antonio, please. Let's talk—"

He sped the car forward and around a turn, barely stopping to drop me in front of my house. "Get out."

I waited for him to change his mind. Maybe if I reached out to touch him, he would relent, but he seemed so radioactive that I couldn't. I took the phone he'd given me from my bag and handed it to him.

"I don't want it," he said, still not looking at me. "Give it to the poor. Just go."

I was a coward. I couldn't fight for him. I didn't know how. I got out, and though I didn't look back, I didn't hear him pull away until I was safely inside.

***

My house was empty. Every surface gleamed. The dishes were put away. The broken swans were gone.

I stepped out of my shoes and looked around for any sign of Katrina. She'd left a few old-style bobby pins, but everything else was gone. She'd always kept most of her stuff at her parents', I reminded myself. I had a family. I could call any of them. And what would I say? They'd walked me through Daniel. Would they walk me through another man? One I couldn't talk about?

I put the phone he'd given me by the charger, and it blooped with an auto update to the music library. Tapping and scrolling, I found he'd left me music ages ago, before I'd squeezed a trigger. Puccini, Verdi, Rossini. Antonio liked opera, and it didn't matter that I liked it too.

I put on *Ave Maria* and shuffled the rest. Went to the refrigerator, didn't open it. The sink, empty. Back around the kitchen.

I made a third and fourth circuit around the island, as if spooling my pain around it. Antonio, my beautiful, brutal capo. He wanted me to be clean, and I'd sullied myself, debased myself, not with sex but violence. I was supposed to be his escape, and I'd walked into a trap where I was empowered to commit murder. For all intents and purposes, I had.

And there were witnesses. People who didn't like or trust me. They'd pat him on the back and tell him to move on to a woman who knew her place. To get cunning and hard and live, or stay gentle and die. A woman who knew the rules. A woman from his world. He'd whisper *mi amore* in her cheek while he held her. He'd make her eggs and protect her innocence with his life.

All of his sweetness would go to her. All of his brutality would stay at the job.

Chapter 37.

My face hurt. I remembered the feeling from when I found Daniel's texts. I iced my face, broke out a new toothbrush, and went the fuck to work. Shit, I'd done this before. I was an old hand. I wasn't going to shake off Antonio that day, and maybe not that week. But I had to, didn't I?

Despite my game face and strong words of self-reliance, Pam saw right through me.

"What happened?" she asked.

"Nothing."

"Uh-huh."

"Can you get me a meeting with Arnie?" I asked. "Fifteen minutes. Tell him it's urgent."

"Don't forget your eleven thirty with Daniel Brower."

I noticed she didn't call him a dickhead, and I raised an eyebrow. Pam stared at me, and I looked over her shoulder. I recognized the faces on her computer screen.

Two mug shots. Bruno Uvoli and Vito from the valet service. I leaned in. Vito's mug shot was for an arrest for the sexual assault of an eleven-year-old girl. Bruno's DNA had been found at the scene of his cousin's death, ten years earlier. No charges.

They'd been shot down assassination style in an abandoned suburban house in Palmdale. They'd just been found, but it was assumed they'd been killed the previous afternoon.

Antonio. All I could think about was Antonio assassinating two men and finding out I'd almost done the same.

"Miss Drazen?" Pam sounded concerned.

"Did you get me Arnie?"

"Ten fifteen. Are you all right? You turned white as a sheet."

"I'm going to go catch up on my email. Hold my calls."

I didn't check my emails at all. I wrote Arnie a short, concise letter of resignation. I was done wasting my life with anything I didn't love.

***

Arnie kept me far longer than fifteen minutes, trying to work out consultancies and flexible hours, more pay, a promotion, a new title. He asked me where I was going. When I said, "Nowhere," he believed me and wished me luck in the most sincere voice I'd ever heard him use.

I saw Daniel's team before I saw him: a handful of men in suits huddled by the window and a woman I recognized. Short, slim, with a professional dark bob, and sensible shoes. Clarice. From her outfit, no one would ever guess she liked being called a filthy whore while sucking a taken man's cock.

I felt absolutely nothing about her presence, and that was a relief in itself.

"Hi, everyone," I said as I approached. "I'm ready. Who's joining me?"

"Just me," Daniel said. "It's my only chance to get rid of these guys."

Clarice grimaced in a valiant attempt at a smile. I led Daniel into the glass conference room where Antonio had threatened to kiss me in front of everyone. We sat at a corner of the desk, me at the head and him at the side.

"You rang?" I said.

"How are you?" he asked. "Besides in no mood for small talk."

"I'm fine. I see you hired Clarice back."

"She was the best speechwriter I ever had. I figured if you weren't coming back to me..."

"Makes sense." It did. It made all the sense in the world. "I'd prefer it if you didn't tell her about anything about what happened between us or about my relationships."

"You said it was over with you and Spinelli."

"So? She has a big mouth, and every thought she's ever had is on her face."

He sighed. "Yeah, I know. Honestly, there's no pillow talk because there's no pillow. I have no time right now for any of it. Did you see the latest polling?"

"Heard about it."

"It's partly Clarice," he said. "She knows her job. But it's also taking action against crime. Caution doesn't play. That's a fact."

"I would have talked you out of it."

"Yeah, well, there you have it."

I didn't realize I was still attached to my work on his campaign until that underhanded non-insult. "Ouch, Dan."

"I'm sorry. I didn't come here to give you a hard time."

"Oh, good."

He leaned forward, getting into his business posture. I saw that his fingernails were cleanly cut, and his hair didn't flop, and his hands didn't seek purchase on old habits or tics.

"You left some notes behind with Bill and Phyllis," he said. "You had a lot of questions about a cluster of buildings in Mount Washington. They brought it to my attention a couple of days ago."

I remembered how to tamp down my emotions and how to control my expression. "I didn't find anything. That's why I didn't bring it up."

"I know. But some of that property was managed by a law firm with one client who was killed by the current owner," he said.

"You lost me on the killing part."

"I'm going to let a judge decide that. In the meantime, I'm getting together a warrant. I wanted to let you know ahead of time. If you left a tube of lipstick there, or a tampon or whatever, you'd better go get it."

I laughed a little to let him know what I thought of his warning.

"What?" he asked.

"You're protecting me?"

"Yes, I am."

"They're not going to forget Catholic Charities. The press might have brushed it off as an interesting photo op of nothing, but if my stuff is on that property, dots get connected. How would it look if it comes out that you sat on your hands for almost a month while a war started? It's going to look like you swept it under the rug because I was involved."

He set his face in a look he'd never given me before. It lacked any compassion or grace. It was the look that scared witnesses. "I want to be clear, so I'm only saying this once. This is the last time I will speak to you as an insider. This is your last concession. If I need to subpoena you, I will. If you have a shred of DNA over there, remove it, because once I walk out of here, I won't hesitate to drag you down with him."

I stood and held out my hand. "Thank you for your consideration, Mister Brower."

Instead of shaking it, he held my face and kissed my right cheek then my left. Though Daniel was as American as apple pie, it felt like a final good-bye.

Chapter 38.

Did I have hours? Days? Was the time between now and Daniel's warrant measured in minutes? And what did I want to do about it?

I put the top down on my dented car as I drove home, as if the extra smog intake would clear my head. But the 10 freeway at rush hour was no place to get my head together.

Antonio had dumped me in no uncertain terms. I owed him nothing. If he got dragged into a black and white tomorrow, it would have nothing at all to do with me. But that image of him in cuffs, for anything, made me pull off onto Crenshaw.

I still had his phone. I swallowed my pride and dialed, heart pounding from the first ring, then the second, then the voicemail announcement. I hung up. I didn't know if I was being ignored or if some smaller insult was being hurled, and I didn't want to think about it.

I plugged the phone into my stereo and listened to Puccini. Could I call East Side Motors? Should I just go? It was about five fifteen. The drive would take me a good forty minutes.

I headed east. When I passed downtown, I'd decide.

***

I saw smoke on the horizon as I went east on the 10. Wildfires were a fact of Southern California life, especially at points north and east of Los Angeles, so I thought nothing of it. Then the traffic on Figueroa was diverted to Marmion, and I heard sirens and saw flashing lights on the flats, not the wooded hills. I parked and walked a block south and two east, smoke choking me. A crowd had gathered at the curb, and the police were hard-pressed to keep them safe from their own curiosity.

"There are underground gas tanks," one cop said to a guy who wanted to cross the street. "They blow, and you're gonna be grease. So get back."

The man got back, and I stepped in his place for half a second to confirm what I knew to be true. East Side Motors was up in flames.

I walked to my car. I knew where Antonio's house was, more or less, but it was very close to the shop, and the fire trucks had blocked off that street. He wasn't getting out without being seen, and neither was I.

I scrolled through my phone, the one without Puccini and Verdi. Did I have Paulie's number? Zo's? Would any of them listen to me or would they just be relieved I was gone? I needed someone I could trust. Someone who had an emotional enough connection to Antonio that I could count on their loyalty.

I felt fit to burst. I needed to tell Antonio what Daniel had told me. I didn't need to make sure I didn't have any tissues at his house. I didn't need to clear myself of malfeasance. I needed to make sure I'd done everything to get him out of the way.

It occurred to me late, almost too late. Too late for me to claim innocence.

I was bait. I was doing exactly what I was supposed to do: going to Antonio and leading the authorities right to him.

"Daniel, you fucking bastard."

I'd never felt so used, so whored in my life. I drove away as fast as I could with the top down, west on Marmion. Was my phone tracked? Who knew what Daniel had done while we were together. If he felt no compunction in tracking my credit card purchases, why wouldn't he track my phone?

At a red light, I wrote down a number from my call history then tossed the thing in a bus stop garbage can. It smacked against the back of the wire mesh and dropped onto a pile of ketchup-covered fast food bags.

I unplugged Antonio's phone and called the number at the next light. If his phone wasn't secure, I didn't know what would be.

"Hello?"

"Marina? This is Theresa Drazen. I'd like to meet with you."

She barked a laugh. "About what? I told you he'd never be with you."

My heart jumped into my throat, as if deciding it needed to be eaten rather than tolerate this. I swallowed hard. "It's business."

"I'm not in the business."

"That's why I want to talk to you."

She didn't answer right away. "What then?"

"It's not what you think. Where is good for you?"

"Dunno. Things are a little crazy with the men right now."

"I know. I'm on Marmion, if that helps."

"Yeah," she said sharply, as if coming to a decision. "Sure, yeah. Come by Yes Café, off La Carna. Ten minutes."

"Thank you."

She didn't hear me apparently, because she'd hung up.

Chapter 39.

Yes Café had plastic-wrapped sandwiches and lousy coffee. The half and half came in little plastic cups with peel tops. I sat in the wooden chair and looked out the window and playing with Antonio's phone. It felt like reminiscing about Antonio, even though the thing was clean of anything but music and a short call history. He'd given it to me, he'd left me, and now it was all I had.

I read the local paper, which reported the same things as the bigger papers: The spate of violence in the city. Bruno Uvoli's nasty history which may or may not have included having a hand in the death of his cousin, Domenico Uvoli. Vito Oliveri's penchant for young girls. Nothing new but the insinuation that they had it coming.

Marina was twenty minutes late. She came in from the parking lot in the back, all heels and tight jeans, makeup and shiny hair. I hadn't realized how young she was, maybe her early twenties. Dew hung on her like the morning, and I felt a twist of jealousy for the fact that she was so fresh and pretty.

"Hi," she said, clutching her purse strap over her shoulder.

"I'm sorry to bother you."

She shrugged and sat. "It's fine."

"Did you tell Antonio you were coming to meet me?"

She looked at me sheepishly.

"It's fine either way," I said.

"I gotta go soon, so if you want to say something?"

I took a deep breath. "I trust you to bring this to Antonio because you care about him."

"He won't like me getting involved."

"I know. He can take it out on me if he wants." I leaned forward, hands folded. "I happen to know that the district attorney is getting a warrant to search *l'uovo.*"

She looked down, shifting her mouth to one side.

I continued. "I don't know when he's serving it. Tonight, tomorrow, next week. So if you could tell Antonio personally as soon as you can."

"Well, the shop is kinda burning down. And uh, I hear things got hot with some of the other guys. The other, um, group."

She was so unpracticed, so raw in her immaturity, I didn't know whether to feel threatened or sorry for her naïveté.

"You seem different than you were on the phone the other night," I said.

She turned pink. "You're intimidating in person."

"Well, in the interest of not making you any more uncomfortable, I have nothing else." I picked up my bag.

"Wait," she said. "You need to tell him what you told me. I don't even know what you're talking about. Do you have a little time?"

Did I? Was I looking to get involved even more deeply? By a woman who perceived me as a threat? Did I want to go home to my empty loft? Or start the round of calls to friends and family to ensure I had things to do and places to go for the next few days? Or did I want to exist in Antonio's sphere for another hour?

"Sure," I said.

***

She drove up the hill in her Range Rover. I followed her lights on the unlit roads. We were a few miles west of the car shop. She stopped on the top of a hill. The concrete ditch of the L.A. River was beneath us.

"This it?" I said.

Below were makeshift shacks occupied by the homeless, some more complex than others. Across the river was Frogtown, but no one would walk across the muck of a dry river bed for that.

"Marina?" I turned to ask her where we were going but stopped short.

She was holding a little silver gun.

"Jesus Christ." I held up my hands.

"What did you do?" she asked. "Tell me. What did you do to make him love you?"

"He doesn't—"

"You're *lying*. He does. You made him crazy. He's still crazy."

"I didn't do anything Marina, I—"

"He's destroyed everything because of you. First, he dumped me, then he threw Vito Oliveri under the bus. And Bruno? Bruno was a good guy. But he saw what was happening, and he tried to get you so he could put some sense into Antonio. It was just going to be an example."

"He let Bruno live, Marina. I was there. He could have killed him. He had his wits about him."

"Bruno was *made*, you dumb Irish bitch. He can't kill him without warning every other family in Los Angeles he's gonna do it. They're coming from the old country to kill Antonio, and now I'm going to save him by killing you. The cause of it all."

I didn't know if it actually worked like that. I wasn't in her world. Maybe if she brought my head to Donna Maria Carloni and whoever was coming from the old country, that would be helpful to Antonio. Maybe the spell I'd woven around him would be broken and he'd start making coherent decisions again.

I stepped back, hands still raised. "You understand if you murder me, you'll go to jail. Is that what you want?"

"For him, I'd go." She straightened her arms and aimed for my heart.

Smart girl, unfortunately. It was a safer shot than the head. Her hands tightened. I would be dead in a second. I wasn't sure my arm would reach when I extended it for the gun. She moved, bending her elbows, and it went off with a flash and a pop.

I didn't feel any pain, just a pressure and a blank space in my thoughts. The world went sideways, then I heard another crack, and—nothing.

Chapter 40.

The pain came first, as if someone had put a sharp clamp on the side of my head. The sounds came afterward. People shuffling, metallic clacking noises, short laughs, all men. The acoustics indicated I was in a small space. And the smell was wet, sticky earth.

My mouth was dry, and I moved my tongue.

"What's the date?" said a voice. *That* voice.

I didn't know the answer, but I opened my eyes. Lights and colors were blurred as if thrown into a blender.

"What's your name?"

"Contessa," I croaked.

"Good."

I blinked, squeezed my eyes shut, and opened them again. The room was tight and low, with dirt walls and ceiling. Enzo and Niccolo passed by, yammering in Italian, and over me was...

"Capo."

"Shh. Please. You got a good knock on the head."

"Where am I?"

"Under *l'uovo*. But I'll say no more."

"Where's Marina?"

He shook his head. "She's fine, but stupid. Otto found her and you just in time. She's being sent home to Naples tomorrow. How is your ear?"

That must be the searing pain on the side of my head. "Hurts."

"It caught a bullet."

I got up on my elbows and looked around. I saw a door on each side of the room and a wall lined with racks of rifles.

"I wanted to tell you something," I said.

"Marina told me."

I noticed then that he wasn't touching me. He wasn't holding my hand or stroking my cheek. His fingers were laced together between his legs.

"Thank you. The warning about the DA is very helpful. We were clearing out anyway. Paulie's gone."

"Why?"

"Why? He put you in a terrible position. We, ah..." He looked at his hands. My vision had cleared enough to see the red scratches on his fists. "We fought. He set the shop on fire. I don't know who he will align with, if anyone. But not me." He stood. The ceiling wasn't much higher than his head.

"Antonio," I said, "where are you going?"

"I have a war to prepare for. Otto will make sure you get home safely." He walked toward the door like a doctor satisfied the patient would live.

"No," I said, suddenly lucid. "Don't. Please."

"Nothing's changed, Theresa."

"That's right." I swung my feet around, and they found the floor. I was sitting on a wooden bench. "Nothing has changed. You feel the same. Deny it. Deny you love me."

"I don't love you."

"You're lying."

"Contessa—"

"Don't call me that until you admit how you feel."

He closed the door, shutting out the sounds of the men. "What difference would it make? I won't destroy you. If I take you in, you'll be miserable. You'll spend your life never knowing who I am or what I do. You'll have to accept that I may go to jail for years, and you can't leave me, even then. It won't be tolerated. That's the better scenario."

"And the worse one?"

"You learn to tolerate me." He put his hand on the doorknob.

I knew that if he went into the other room, only Otto would come back. It would be the last I'd see of him. So I jumped up and stood in front of the door. The world swam. I tried to lean on the wall, but my stomach turned over, and I was sure I would fall.

Antonio's arms went around me, holding me up. My senses came back, and I pushed him away.

"Admit you love me." I touched his face, feeling the stubble on his cheek and the exhaustion emanating from him. I wanted to make it all go away, to give him peace.

"It wouldn't make any difference," he said.

"Admit it."

"I loved you the second I put my eyes on you. It doesn't matter."

"Let me love you back."

"You have a life to live."

"I have nothing." I stroked his lip, and his hands remained at his sides. "I've danced enough. I've seen movies. I've been in every pool in Malibu. I've travelled. I've dated. Worked on a political campaign. Met stars. Had a job. I've done all that. What I've never done is love a man like you."

He turned, ever so slightly, and kissed my palm, letting his eyes close. "What if you die from loving me?"

"What if I die from not loving you?"

He kissed my cheek, and I melted into him. I thought I'd never feel those lips again, and when I did, I groaned.

"Please," I whispered. "I'll follow you anywhere."

"You're going to get hurt."

"Hurt me, then. I'd rather get hurt than live a lie."

He put his forehead to mine and wove his hands behind my neck. It increased the pain in my head, but I fell into it, wanting his pain as much as I wanted his pleasure.

"Contessa, you make me crazy."

"I know."

"I don't know where you'll fit in with me. I don't know your place."

"My place is beside you."

He leaned back, and I felt the loss of his touch deeply. I needed more. But he put his hand behind his collar and took off his medal of St. Christopher.

He pressed it into my palm, one hand over mine, one under. He looked into my face as if watching a storm gather. The metal was hard on my skin and warm from being close to him.

"Are you sure you want to never feel safe?" he asked. "Are you sure you want to always look behind you? Are you sure you want a life without people you trust?"

"If you're with me, yes."

"Are you sure you can love a man who's damned?"

"Only you. Damned or saved, I want only you."

"I have a problem, my Contessa. It's been eating me alive since I kissed you. I want you, and I don't know how to have you. I want you beside me. I want my world and your world to be one. To see you laugh in the morning. To see you weep my name at night. I am not ever afraid, but with you, I am. I'm afraid I won't have you, and I'm afraid I will."

He turned my hand over until my palm was facing downward, clutching the medal. He leaned down and kissed it, fingers, knuckles, wrist, and looked up at me. His eyes were felony black, lips built for declarations of love, jaw set to break barriers.

"I can't let you go," he said. "I want to be that man who can make you breakfast and raise children without always looking behind his back. I am going to make myself worthy. I am going to get out so I can't hurt you. But I can't just walk away from what I do, and I can't turn away from you. God help me, every time I walk away from you, I only see hell in front of me."

I put my hands on his face, letting the chain slip over my thumb and dangle. "Don't walk away from me. It kills me when you do."

"This life, it's impossible to pay every debt and go straight."

"Pay what you can."

He took the chain and opened it. I leaned into him so he could put it around my neck and fasten it.

I laid my head on his shoulder and pulled back. "Ow. My ear."

He turned my head to get a good look. "It's barely a scratch." He kissed my neck, moving the chain to put his tongue on the skin where my neck and shoulder met.

"I have a headache," I said, pushing his ass forward until I felt his erection at my hip.

"I'll fuck you gently. You'll come long and slow. Your head will forget its ache when you shed tears." He reached under my skirt from behind.

I groaned.

"Shh," he said. "My men are on the other side of this door." He pushed me back onto the bench and spread my legs. *"Mi amore."*

He kissed inside my thighs, moving my panties aside to lick so slowly I almost came with anticipation. I grabbed his hair, but he wouldn't suck. He only used the tip of his tongue on my clit.

"Antonio," I whispered. The hard bench bit my back and the room was rough hewn from the earth, yet I'd never felt so comfortable, at home, safe. "Always be my Capo."

He slid my underpants off and planted himself between my legs, his dick out and ready for me.

"What do you want?" he asked.

"Fuck me," I said with conviction. "Fuck me now."

He put one of my legs over his shoulder, opening me for him. He moved my body like a precious thing, then he slid his dick into me. I was so wet, he got the whole length of him in with one try.

"Come vuoi tu, Contessa." He moved out then in again, every inch a breath of intention to keep me safe, to keep me pure. But most importantly, I felt his intention to keep me. His voice dropped, and his words sounded more like prayer than surrender. *"Come vuoi tu."*

Fine, per adesso.

Thank you for reading.

I anticipate two more in the series, and I may need up to six months between them.

The best way to find out when the next book is out is to sign up for my mailing list at cdreiss.com.

My email is cdreiss.writer@gmail.com.

****

Thanks to my team, Cassie, Lynn, the Canaries, Team Drazen, all my goddesses and kings for making 2013 my most creative and rewarding. Kaylee, Jean, Lisa, Tony, Diana, Eva, Christy. I'm a slobbering idiot without you.

Gabri Canova helped with the Italian phrasing in the story. Thank you, Goddess.

Erik Gevers did the formatting, yet again making me look like a pro.

My family tolerates me. D-Sleepy, A-Bomb, Lady Nono.